THE HOLE

IN THE

SKY

PORTAL ONE

By

Karen B. Crumley

Also by Karen Crumley

Weapon of Jihad

Growing Up Weird:

Confessions of a Closet

Medium

THE HOLE

IN THE

SKY

PORTAL ONE

Purple Sage Publishing

2017

A Special Thanks

to

Kathy B.

and

Pat Smith

THE HOLE IN THE SKY: PORTAL ONE

Copyright @ 2017 by Karen Crumley at Purple Sage Publishing

Cover art and design by Purple Sage Publishing

Purple Sage Publishing, PO Box 1431, Goldthwaite, Texas 76844

Blog   http://theholeintheskysite.wordpress.com

LCCN PCN   2017939519

ISBN-13:
978-0983669036 (Purple Sage Publishing)
ISBN-10:
0983669031

Ephesians 6:12
For we wrestle not against flesh and
blood, but against principalities,
against powers, against the rulers of
the darkness of this world, against
spiritual wickedness in high places.

Genesis 28:12
And he dreamed, and behold a ladder
set up on the earth, and the top of it
reached to heaven: and behold the
angels of God ascending and
descending on it.

THE HOLE

IN THE

SKY

PORTAL ONE

THE HOLE IN THE SKY: PORTAL ONE

CHAPTER 1

The rumble of the old Dodge pickup truck intensified into a hum as Luke shifted into third gear. The only time he remembered that he needed to have that muffler replaced was when he was driving down the road. The shadows of the mesquite trees and the creeping cold reminded him that the sun was rapidly sinking down behind him.

He usually started his evening rounds on the ranch much earlier, but the two beers he sipped with his lunch had drugged him into a stupor that he could not pull out of until a few minutes ago. He pressed the pedal a little harder at the thought. If he did not hurry, he would not be able to check the water.

His own tardiness angered him. He needed to find his dogs, Ben and Bertha, who sat out among his herd of sheep and guarded them. The huge, white forms of the two Great Pyrenees hampered the attacks of the coyotes on his sheep. God knew how many sheep those dogs had saved for him. He had only witnessed their fierce attack once. It made him almost feel sorry for that coyote, but not really.

He took each of the dogs a can of dog food every day. They always wagged their tails and ran up eagerly to greet Luke in anticipation of their treat. They were more than just dogs... they were friends. Luke had decided that having dogs as companions was much easier than being married. He never needed to worry that they would cheat on him. But, he had not seen them for two days and now he was worried. What could possibly happen to two of the strongest dogs in the world? The gears complained loudly as Luke slowed down to turn into the ranch.

"Dang it all!" The sun was already beginning to set and spooky shadows grew longer and darker around him as he opened the truck door and stepped around to open the gate. He zipped his brush jacket closed and twirled the numbers on the combination lock until it gave way. Then, he pushed the gate open. The hinges on the gate screamed a new squeal and a group of coyotes wailed off in the distance at the same time.

"Darn! When did that start? I gotta remember the silicone spray," he said out loud, partly just to hear the sound of his own voice after the gate's unsettling screech. He stepped back into his truck and closed the door quickly behind himself.

"Come off it, Luke... stop the heebie-jeebies!" He finally resorted to clicking on his lights so he could follow the old, rutted-out dirt road. The lights jumped up and down as the road tossed the truck in all directions.

"Gonna have to get a dozer in here." Controlling the wagging steering wheel, Luke squinted, hoping to see any sign of his dogs. A frown crossed his brow.

"So, why don't I see any sheep either?" He raised his eyebrows in hope. Maybe that meant the dogs and the sheep were all together somewhere. A patch of white suddenly caught his eye to his left. It was a sheep... a very dead sheep.

"What in tarnation happened to you?" The pickup kept creeping down the road until the forms of three more sheep—dead sheep—came into view.

"That's it! What happened here?" He slammed on the brakes and threw the truck into neutral. Jumping out of the truck, he grabbed his Q-beam and headed to the carcasses. Caked blood covered the wool and told the story of a vicious attack. Curiously enough, though, none of the carcasses had been eaten in any way. Something just murdered them and left them there.

"Darn! Gonna hafta get the trapper out here! What could have done this?" The coyotes had always been a problem, but they made characteristic kills. A coyote slashed the blood vessels in the throat and the victim bled to death. This... this was different. Probing the heads and necks of the sheep, Luke realized that something had grabbed the head and crushed down on the skull... something with massive, strong jaw muscles. His eyes glanced all around. He caught a glimpse of something dark like a shadow gliding toward a wide sage bush.

"Great...now I'm imagining things!" He turned his attention back to the slaughtered sheep. "That ain't no coyote kill!"

He kicked rocks as he walked back to the truck and threw the Q-beam onto the passenger seat. He slammed the door shut and crept forward in second gear. He passed first two, then three more slaughtered sheep. The farther he went, the more he found. He could see that they all died the same way. Some of the carcasses were eviscerated and silvery intestines stretched out all around them. But nothing had been eaten.

Sick to his stomach now, Luke pushed the truck forward. Everywhere he looked, the glazed eyes of the mutilated sheep stared back at him.

"Oh, my God! The whole flock?" He frowned as his mood turned sour. God did not have anything to do with this. He was beginning to wonder if God had anything to do with anything. His recent life reflected the same pattern of disastrous loss. After twelve years of marriage, his wife left him for an accountant. He never understood women and he now doubted that any woman existed who could understand him. He would go through the rest of his miserable existence alone. It was better than suffering through that pain again. And now, he could lose his ranch because of this huge loss. Where was God? Fear and dread overwhelmed him until...he saw something out of the corner of his eye.

"Is that a sheep?" He swung his Q-beam to the left to get a good look and held his breath. Draped almost ceremoniously across a mesquite bush was another sheep. It hung upside-down and its legs were all spread out like it had been crucified. Luke's mouth hung open in his attempt to comprehend the sight as the truck crept forward without him noticing. Suddenly, a jolt pulled Luke out of his shock. He slammed on the brakes. What did he run over? He jumped out of the truck with his Q-beam. It was Bertha! Bertha lay in the road bearing the same wounds as the sheep.

"Naw... naw... that can't be... nothin could do that to B..." and he began to sob. Bertha was his friend.

"Ah, Bertha, what happened to you?" He looked around. "And where is Ben?" Suddenly he heard a low noise to his right. Could it be Ben? He swung the Q-beam in that direction and saw...

Ben. No, Ben's body. Sobbing uncontrollably now, he stumbled over to it.

"Naw, Naw... not you too! Ah! God, what happened?"

He heard the low noise again. He knew it was not Bertha or Ben. He took a breath and swung his Q-beam to scan the area. Hot breath sent flumes of warm air into the cold, creating a surreal mist as his mind grappled with the meaning of the sight. Suddenly, a mass of glowing eyes met the beam at the same time the sound of horrendous growling sent chills down his spine. It was a pack of coyotes... only not coyotes. Massive heads and colossal jaws baring huge canines snarled at Luke.

He froze. His mind tried to analyze what he was seeing, but it made no sense. Everything went into slow motion. These were coyotes, but coyotes do not run in packs. Coyotes do not have massive heads or jaws. Coyotes do not have alpha leaders. These did.

His size distinguished the Alpha from the rest of the pack. He stood about a foot taller than the rest of them, and his legs bulged with muscle, giving him a slight bowlegged look. He glared and snarled at Luke, almost smiling. Then, he took one step forward.

In one panicked motion, Luke swung around and headed for the truck, his feet slipping on spinning pebbles. His left hand grabbed the grill guard, aiding his scramble around the truck to the safety of its door. Leaping into the seat, he slammed the door shut... and just in time.

Loud thuds announced the arrival of the coyotes behind him only microseconds later. They hurled their bodies at the truck in some kind of crazed attempt to break through the metal. Claws scratched deeply into the roof of the truck, and then something really heavy caused the front of the truck to sink down.

Luke, who had been busy reacting to the coyotes attacking at the side door of the truck, turned to see why the truck tilted. His mouth fell open. There, on the hood in front of him, the Alpha perched, glaring through the windshield at Luke. His eyes still glowed, even though Luke's spotlight was not shining on them. He took small, menacing steps toward the windshield, even as other coyotes gnawed on the side mirrors. The sounds of gnawing, growling and metal giving in to the blows of the coyotes blended now with a new sound. The Alpha scraped his oversized canines on the windshield like a glass cutter, making a high-pitch scream.

His eyes fixed on the Alpha, Luke reached to the back of the seat for his rifle, but he could not find it with his searching hand. He tore his gaze from the fiery eyes of the Alpha to look back and locate it. There it was. He grabbed it like it was his best friend and slid off the safety as he pulled it over the seat to aim it at the Alpha.

But the Alpha was gone.

And so were all of the other coyotes.

With the rifle still in his shaking hand, Luke just sat there for a few minutes in the dead silence.

"What in the Hell…!" It was all he could say.

So, he said it a couple more times.

CHAPTER 2

Dana Fleming closed the door behind her after the last student walked into class. The ugly mood of the students today was obvious, even in the hall. Sarah and Brandon had been a couple now for at least a year, but today they were fighting loudly in the hall over which car to take on their date. Dana had never seen them have a single cross word with each other.

Then there was Armand. Dana came around the corner just in time to see Armand lunge at Whitney and the resulting fight. So, it took her a little longer to get to class because she had to escort the two boys to the office.

So, Dana began to write on the board.

"Time after class... in minutes (it was important to model proper use of units):____"

She went ahead and filled in a one in the blank and the class let out a collective moan.

"You know you're supposed to be quiet in the hall when you're waiting on me."

"But Misssss!"

"I don't know what's gotten into you today, but it's got to stop now! If you think I'm going to let you into the lab the way you're behaving now, you're wrong." She frowned at the now silent, glaring class. They loved to get into the lab. "Do you think you can behave back there?"

"Yes Ma'am...," the class answered in a disappointed unison.

"Ok... then we'll give it a try... but I'll be watching."

The students put on their goggles and aprons and formed groups in the lab area. Dana walked along beside the tables watching every move. One of the students stepped out to ask Dana a question.

Amy's short, blond hair was tied up in a knot, somehow intertwined with her goggles. Teachers were not supposed to have favorites, but, if it were allowed, Amy would be one of Dana's favorites. She was also a friend of her daughter, Lola.

"Mrs. Fleming, I was wondering if Lola can come to a slumber party I'm having for my birthday next week. It will be next Saturday. My parents will be there." Lola must have been spreading unreasonable mother stories about her to her friends for Amy to take such care in telling her about the fact that her parents would be there.

Dana smiled. "I think that would be alright, Amy." Amy lived out on a ranch not too far away from where Dana lived.

"Mrs. Fleming?"

"Yes."

"Do you have a headache?"

Dana had been too busy to realize it. "Yes, I do. Why?"

"Because you're frowning like you have a headache."

"Oh... I didn't know it was that obvious."

"I hope you feel better Mrs. Fleming."

"Oh... thanks Amy." Well, the approaching front must be getting to her, too. Come to think of it, Dana had noticed that everybody was grouchy.

Only, it could not be the approaching front causing it because it had been increasing for several weeks. It made her feel jumpy.

Crash! As if on cue, a beaker hit the floor and shattered into a million pieces. The whole class turned toward the ruckus.

"Uh, Miss...nobody touched it. It fell off by itself!"

Dana thought for a moment. "The table was probably wet and it just slid off. Just clean it up and put it in the broken glass container."

Heather Corey and Alexis Gomez turned to each other and shrugged. They waited until Dana walked away and began to carefully clean up the mess. "But it was dry," Heather whispered under her breath.

Alexis frowned and looked down. "Yeah, I know."

"So how did it get knocked off? We were nowhere near it and it was a good two feet away from the edge."

"I don't know. That's just creepy."

"Uhmm, Alexis? Did you see what I saw?"

"If you're talking about that shadow, no. I don't believe in those things."

"Uhmm, yeah. But I would still like to know how that happened."

Dana saw the two girls whispering. "Everything okay over there?"

"Yes, Miss," they both said.

Dana shook her head. She hoped the ugly mood from the front would pass soon. It was getting to everybody. Everybody except... the Watchers.

The Watchers belonged to a certain family in town. Their mentally challenged parents worked hard to raise their three sons, who had inherited the condition. Dwayne and Donny attended classes with everyone else and they performed as well as possible, never causing any trouble. In fact, their behavior exemplified how respectful teenagers should behave. But this week they unnerved Dana. They had not done anything particularly bad. Maybe what bothered her was the way the arrival of the cold front did not affect them like the other students. The look in their eyes seemed to laugh at all the other students. How curious. But they were always a little different.

Dana called them 'The Watchers' only in her thoughts. She had noted something about this family. They all watched. They lived along a very busy street in the small town. Any time of day or night that a person drove by, one of the family members stood outside in the front yard by the street watching. They smiled and waved at everyone. While the sons attended class at high school, the parents took over the watching but as soon as the school day ended, the sons began their watching duty on the street.

CHAPTER 3

Billy LaGioia scratched his balding head and took a deep breath as he surveyed the sight before him. He would have expected this if he was raising goats or sheep, but it made no sense because he was raising cattle. He knew the neighbors had coyote problems and he had heard someone talking about sighting a mountain lion. But this was not the work of coyotes or mountain lions. The tracks were cat tracks, but not mountain lion tracks. Billy knew bobcat tracks when he saw them and he knew the tracks in front of him were made by many bobcats. He scratched his head again. Bobcats were supposedly solitary animals and this made no sense.

Walking up to the carcass, he kicked a caliche rock away from its head. He bent down to get a closer look at the wounds on the body of the steer in front of him. Bites covered the legs of the unfortunate animal and it was obvious that several animals had participated in the kill by all of the different-sized paw prints in the soil around it. The abdomen had been ripped open and the internal organs had been devoured.

As he crouched near the kill, he thought he saw something out of the corner of his eye. He quickly glanced up to get a better look, but it was gone. He thought he saw something black slide silently into the brush. He shook his head and rubbed his eyes.

"Now I'm seeing things."

He stood up, brushed the dirt off his hands and zipped his coat. Then he raised his eyes up to the sky.

"God....you have to help me here. If you don't, I'm done." He looked back down at the carcass.

"Bobcats do not kill steers," he uttered audibly as if to repeat something he had learned before. And yet, bobcats had apparently ripped this steer to death. He would have felt better if he had seen mountain lion tracks because that would have fit all he had learned through years of ranching.

"What kind of bobcat goes after a grown steer? That's it. I'm calling Ignacio...and he'd better have an answer for this." He fumbled in his pocket for his phone, found his contact list and selected the one that said 'trapper'. He waited until he heard Ignacio's voice.

"Hey Ignacio, I thought you told me that you had these bobcats under control. I just found a grown steer killed by bobcats last night."

Ignacio frowned. "That's impossible. You know bobcats can't do that. Are you sure it's not a mountain lion kill?"

"Positive! There are bobcat tracks all over around it and not one lion track."

"Hmmm. I'll get out there at have a look. Was it eaten?"

"Yeah. All the guts are gone. Now you know you have to do something about this. I can't afford to lose any more like this. When are you coming?"

"Give me a half an hour."

"Okay. You have to get this stopped!"

Ignacio heard the burning anger and frustration in Billy's voice but what could he do about it? He was sure that he would find lion tracks when he got there.

"Billy just can't tell the difference between bobcat tracks and mountain lion tracks. That's what it is. Bobcats don't kill steers!"

Savannah Massingill gripped the top of the seat in front of her. "C'MON! FASTER!"

April Caldwell frowned, "I am! This car won't go any faster!"

She executed a ninety degree turn, sliding out of control and sending globs of mud flying over her mother's compact car. Savannah and Heather Martin flew to the other side of the back seat in response to the sudden turn.

Savannah grinned as she slid back over to her side of the seat. "That's more like it!"

Heather tapped April's shoulder. "Yeah. Do that again!"

"Sure!" April grimaced and floored the pedal and adjusted her grip on the steering wheel. As she got up to speed, she jerked the steering wheel again and the little car went sliding in the slick mud created by the recent rains. The car slid out of control and all of the girls screamed in horror as it headed towards a small tree.

THUD. The car came to a sudden stop and the girls dropped their mouths open and looked at each other to make sure everybody was okay. April gingerly peaked out her window to get a glimpse of the damage.

"Well?" asked Heather.

April shushed her. "Don't know yet. I don't see anything. I can't get out on this side." She got up on her knees in the seat and crawled over the console between the seats to reach the other door. Then she opened the door and climbed out of the car, nearly falling as she caught herself by sinking her hands into the mud. Without thinking, she wiped her hands on her brand new basketball uniform and then grimaced.

She coiled in disgust. "Ahhhh! I just sank down to my knees in mud!"

Loud peals of laughter followed from the back seat. April lifted up her leg and trudged in front of the car to the driver's side, sinking with each step. The little car rested snugly up against the tree. She bent down and rested her hands on her muddy knees to inspect the damage.

"I can't see anything. We have to get away from the tree. C'mon! Get out!"

"Ughhh. Are you kidding? No way!"

"Well I sure can't pick this car up with your fat butts sitting in it!"

Heather and Savannah looked at each other and laughed.

Heather pushed Savannah and tried to look serious under April's angry stare. "Well, get out Savannah!"

The two girls opened the door and made faces of disgust as they took a deep breath and stepped into the ooze. Now it was April's turn to laugh as she threw mud onto her squeamish friends. Big, brown spots of mud now covered the girls' new basketball uniforms.

"Cut it out!" screamed Savannah as she shielded her face from an oncoming mud glob. "Cut it out! Coach is going to kill us! We just got these uniforms today!"

April bent down to get a grip on the front bumper. "Get over to the back of the car and help me slide it over." The girls each took one side of the back bumper.

"Okay. We're ready."

"On three! One, two, three!" Their faces turned red and their feet slipped in the mud as they strained to move the car a foot away from the tree. April held her hand up to signal them to stop.

"Wait. Let me look!" She began to move through the sludge to the driver side of the car and peered around the fender at the front door.

Savannah stuck her head out the window. "Well?"

"That's just amazing! Not a scratch! The mud must have protected it."

"Whew! You would have had a real problem explaining that to your mom."

"You mean WE would have had a real problem explaining that to my mom! C'mon! Help me get this pointed to the road. We have to get to the car wash."

"And the laundry room!"

"Shhh!" April turned to face the pasture behind her. "Do you hear that?"

"What?"

"Listen! Somebody is screaming."

Heather and Savannah strained their ears with April until the screaming began again. They looked at each other in confusion. Heather frowned. "Who is that?"

April took a step towards the pasture. "That's Genie Nixon's place and it sounds like Genie."

"Who's Genie Nixon and why is she screaming?"

"She's my mother's friend. She has a herd of milk goats and sells goat milk and goat cheese. My mom buys it. I don't know why she's screaming. She sounds like she's being murdered or something! Let's go see what's going on."

The girls straightened the car, jumped in and hurried off in the direction of the ruckus. A back road led to Genie's place and the girls covered it in only minutes. As they approached Genie's home, they saw Genie frantically slinging rocks at something in the brush. Her goats frantically ran around her bleating in panic. April strained to see what hid behind the bushes. Genie never even reacted to their presence. She kept throwing big rocks intently and screaming at whatever hid in the brush.

April ran up to Genie. "Genie! What?!"

"Coyotes! A pack of 'em! They're after my goats. They already killed one over there!"

April glanced over to her left and saw the mutilated body of a goat with a big, red bandana around its neck. Being raised on a ranch, she knew that coyotes killed goats, but not in the light of day and not in the presence of humans. As Genie and the girls stood there, the coyotes began to step out of the brush. What April saw took her by surprise. These coyotes broke all the rules about size. They looked more like wolves than coyotes and they apparently ran in a pack like wolves. Blood matted their fur and their piercing eyes glowed. Yet, April knew they were coyotes because she had seen plenty of them hung up on fences by trappers after they had been killed.

Through the middle of the coyote pack, an enormous coyote stepped forward and snarled menacingly at Genie who stood the closest to it. Genie froze with her arm holding a rock in midair and her mouth fell open in shock at the size of the growling animal facing her. Huge canines flashed in his mouth as his lips curled back and saliva dripped freely. Rotting meat from previous kills lodged in his teeth and emanated a horrific smell as the beast exhaled.

Heather and Savannah reacted to this with a scream in unison. April noticed some tools leaning against the nearby shed and she ran over to grab them. She tossed a hoe to Savannah and a rake to Heather. Then she picked up the axe and began to swing it aggressively as she stomped toward the alpha coyote in a show of strength. "Growl and swing those tools! If you don't, they'll attack us all!"

The girls gave a slight nod and did what April told them to do. The three of them began to stomp towards the coyotes as they growled and swung their weapons. Genie saw this and joined in after grabbing a big cedar post on the ground close to her. The alpha stepped closer and yawned and growled at the same time, a clear threat to his attackers. April knew they needed something else. Then, she remembered.

She shouted, "Keep at it!" as she ran to the car and opened the front passenger door. Reaching in, she opened the glove compartment and pulled out her mom's mace spray. She ran forward to the alpha, yelling at the top of her lungs. As she got close enough, she stopped yelling and held her breath. She sprayed the canister toward the coyotes. The mist of mace, visible now, flew over the pack and the coyotes began to sputter and back off. She kept spraying and then aimed it directly at the alpha who now stopped growling and began to back away also, keeping his intense eyes locked onto April. She stomped her feet. "Get!!! Get!! You heard me....GET!!!!"

Heather, Savannah and Genie took their cue and started stomping and yelling, "GET!!!" The alpha's eyes began to dart around from person to person as it slowly backed into the brush behind him. Suddenly, he stopped backing and leveled a direct glare at April. April glared back. "GET!!!" And then he disappeared into the brush.

Genie and the girls began to cough and tears flowed from their eyes as the mace spray drifted toward them. They backed away from the area as fast as possible, keeping their tearing eyes peeled on the brush.

"We better get these goats into the barn before those monsters decide to come back." Genie staggered to the barn and opened the door as the girls herded the goats inside. "I don't know what would have happened if you girls had not shown up when you did." She led them into her house and offered them a soda. They sat down at the small dining table in Genie's kitchen, still shaken over what had just happened.

"Has this happened before?" April wanted to know more about anything that would stand up to her best forceful act so willingly.

"No. I've never seen anything like those beasts. What were they? Coyotes don't act like that. You suppose they were rabid?"

"No. They weren't confused at all. They had definite purpose." April shuttered at the memory of the defiant stare in the Alpha's eyes. "You gonna be okay?"

Genie took a deep breath. "Yeah, I'm just going to have to carry a gun with me everywhere I go is all. They gave no warning. The only thing I saw was the goats freaking out. Then, there they were....just looking at me like I was their next meal." Still shaking, Genie thanked the girls and sent them home with some of her best goat cheese. As the girls drove away, Genie sat down on the wicker chair on her porch, gripped her twenty-two and closed her eyes tightly.

"Oh, My God....Please protect me!"

CHAPTER 4

Miguel and Francisco struggled to keep up with the others. They followed about ten feet behind the rest of the group. The white plastic jug they had just filled with water weighed much more now and was cumbersome to handle as they walked. And yet, to let go of the water now would be deadly in this dry country. They glanced at each other. All of the men in the group before them had lived many more years than they had. Their relative youth should make them stronger, but they lagged behind the other men.

One of the men turned and faced them. "A compadres! Why are you so slow? Andale! We have to walk across the rest of this county to meet our ride!"

They shifted their jugs to their other hands and quickened their steps. The veterans of this trek continued in a straight path that followed the electric line. Nothing got in their way. They cut two fences that had been repaired since their last journey and kept going at a steady pace.

So when the group before them suddenly cut to the right for no apparent reason, Miguel turned to Francisco in surprise.

"Must be Immigration," Miguel commented to Francisco.

But, as he reached the top of the hill and followed the gaze of the others, he saw no Border Patrol agents. In fact, there was nobody there, just an open field with the greenest grass he had ever seen. It looked inviting to him, so he started to step toward it. Instantly, one of the others caught his arm and pulled him back.

"No... don't go in there."

He looked back at the field, then at the man.

"Why not?"

The rest of the group had now turned to face Miguel. They whispered among themselves, the oldest stepped toward him.

"We don't go in there. Spirits rule this place. We will go around it."

"What? Why? You take us over this land so fast because you say we have to hurry, and now you say we are going around? You make no sense, Old Man!"

He swung around and took three steps into the lush green grass. An eerie, light feeling came over him as the small hairs on the nape of his neck began to stand up. His eyes opened wide and he took a deep breath in surprise. Fear drove him back out of the green area. He stood there staring at it, completely mystified at the feeling he had just had.

"Si, Compadre... Spirits rule this place!" repeated an older man in a gruff voice.

Miguel turned toward the man. "What is that? I have never known anything like that!"

The man nodded upwards toward the sky. "Look over there... look around. Even the rain clouds don't go there."

Sure enough, the clouds covered the sky all around, except over the field. A soft, white beam beaconed onto the grass from the opening in the clouds and a slight mist oozed from the cloud edges.

"It never rains there, but look at the grass... greener than anywhere else."

A somewhat smaller man came up behind Miguel. "And the animals don't go there. No sheep graze there. No insects... nothing."

Miguel just stared at it now. The light was indescribable. It captured his gaze and poured a kind of peace all around.

The old man whispered, "The hole in the sky is always here." He looked up and all around. "It will be dark before long and we do not want to be near here when it gets dark."

"Why not?"

"The lights. Let's go!"

Miguel frowned and slowly shook his head. The older men took off before him as he stood there for a few moments staring at the pasture. Then, he saw something black at the corner of his eye. He turned to look at it but there was nothing there.

"Those old men have really got me spooked!"

CHAPTER 5

Ignacio spotted Billy's truck just down the rutted road from the gate to the ranch and pulled up beside it before he came to a stop and killed the ignition. Billy rose up from the log that had been supporting him as he sat contemplating his bleak future. Ignacio walked toward him and extended his right hand, giving him a concerned look.

"I'm sorry you're having this problem, Billy. Show me what you have."

Billy led Ignacio a few feet away to the location of the kill and shook his head. "This beats all I ever stepped in, Ignacio. Look, it's a mostly-grown steer, for pity sake. I could understand it if it was a mountain lion, but it ain't." He moved closer to the carcass and reached out his finger to point out the bites all over the animal. "This ain't the work of one animal. And look at those tracks.

Ignacio leaned forward over the tracks and he crossed his brow in confusion. Billy was right. Cat tracks of all different sizes littered the area but none of them qualified to be mountain lion tracks. "Huh, I've never seen anything like this before, Billy."

Billy tilted his head to one side as he looked Ignacio in the eye. "What do you mean?"

Ignacio hated to have to admit to Billy that he had never experienced such a situation. Trappers were supposed to be knowledgeable about all possibilities in situations like this. Their expertise kept them employed. He took off his hat and scratched his head. "You're right. These are cat tracks and they're not mountain lion tracks. They look like bobcat tracks and the fact that the kill is partially buried is characteristic of a bobcat. But, these are tracks of many different sized bobcats. They don't hunt together so this makes no sense."

Billy straightened up and waited for Ignacio to do the same. "So, now what?"

"Now we set more traps and see what happens. They'll be back to eat on the kill some more and we'll catch them when they do. I have some traps in my truck so I'll go ahead and set them up."

Billy gave him a hard look. "Well, I hope you figure this out. I can't take any more of this or

I'm done." He shook his head and turned to amble to his truck. "I'm going home. Let me know what you find. Thanks, Ignacio." He turned his truck around through the pasture and drove off on the dirt road to the gate.

Ignacio watched as Billy drove off and then he walked to his truck to look for his #2 Victor traps. Bobcats always return to their meal. With a small shovel, he dug a hole seven inches deep with a seven-inch diameter. Placing the trap into the hole, he carefully covered it with a small bit of cloth. He filled his sifter with the dirt from the hole and now sifted it delicately over the cloth and the surrounding area. He surveyed the scene around the kill. "That should do it."

The next day, Ignacio opened the ranch gate and drove through, wondering what he would find at the site of the kill. Buzzards flew up as he approached, but the fact that he did not hear any sounds of an animal struggling against the metal of the trap told him that he had not caught anything. He moved to the trap, carefully avoiding stepping on any tracks around the kill. The trap had been triggered, but the intended victim had managed somehow to avoid getting caught in it. To add insult, a pile of bobcat scat rested squarely on top of the triggered trap. The dry, well-formed scat held small tufts of hide from the steer nearby.

"So, you want to play hard ball, huh?" Ignacio now strode to his truck and pulled out several more #2 Victor traps. He carefully set them up all around the kill. Someone was bound to hit one of these.

He drove home and pulled off his boots at the door. He grabbed a frozen dinner from the freezer and set it in the microwave to cook. He gathered his utensils and pulled the dinner out when the microwave beeped. Opening the refrigerator door, he grabbed a beer and popped the top as he sat down to his computer with his lunch. He turned the TV on and changed the channel to a wildlife channel. He often watched these shows as he checked his email and ate his lunch. Skimming his email, he found a joke that his friend had forwarded and began to read.

The commentator droned on in the background about the lions and their hunting skills. "Singling out a certain water buffalo, the lions gather around it and coordinate their attack to bring it down."

Ignacio frowned and looked away from the email to listen more intently to the commentator. On the TV screen, a large lion surged from the group and leaped onto the back of the water buffalo as it spun around to defend itself. The lion bit onto the back of her victim's neck and held on firmly as the water buffalo bucked and spun around. The other lions began to join into the attack and bit the beast on its haunches and legs and even on the nose until it fell over. The lions piled onto their victim and began ripping flesh, even as the beast kicked in futility. Soon, the buffalo became still and the lions ripped open its abdomen and ate the liver voraciously. They continued to feed peacefully on their kill.

The commentator continued his explanation. "No single lion could possibly take on the water buffalo successfully. It is the action of the group that brings down a large prey."

Ignacio stopped chewing mid-bite as he intently watched the lions devouring their prey. "That's just like that kill on Billy's place." He pondered a little further and wondered if bobcats could work together like lions to bring down a steer. "Nah! It's got to be some escaped exotic cat, maybe from some wealthy Mexican rancher." He knew of ranchers across the border who kept pet panthers and lions.

He left his lunch sitting and walked to his closet. Leaning over, he pulled a large box out from under the coats. "Okay, let's see what they think about these!"

The next morning, Ignacio loaded his box into the back of his truck and headed to Billy's ranch. As he turned off toward the kill, his mind wandered to the task at hand. The video of the lions ripping the water buffalo apart replayed itself in his mind. Eagerly anticipating finding something in his trap, he maneuvered his way to the kill, only to find he had caught nothing. Once again, a pile of bobcat scat lay ceremoniously placed on top of a triggered trap with no victim.

"How the hell did they do that?" He knew bobcats had been there but he thought they were merely feeding off of a lion kill. All of the traps had been sprung. So Ignacio went to his truck and pulled the box out of the back. "Let's try these babies."

He pulled a Conibear 220 trap out of the box, laid it close to the kill. He drove a stake into the ground through a large ring to secure the trap, then grabbed the scissor setters from the box. Using the scissor setters to compress the springs on one side, he carefully slid the J hook over it to hold it in place. He did the same thing on the other side of the trap. Then, he used the setters to pull the center parts of the trap together and get the J hook loaded onto it. He released the J hooks on both sides and carefully avoided touching the center of the trap as he backed away and wiped the dirt off of his hands. He put his hands on his hips and stood back to look at his work.

He smiled. "Let's see you get around this baby. Better yet, try to take a crap on it!" He had to wonder what he would find the next morning. He drove home and went out to eat with his son, Eric. He tried to explain his problem to Eric.

"I don't know, Eric, it's got me stumped. It looks like a lion kill, but the tracks are bobcat tracks. I'm thinking it's just that the bobcats are feeding off of the lion kill. Still, I haven't seen any tracks big enough to be a mountain lion. And I never knew bobcats to feed together like that."

"Well, you'll know tomorrow maybe."

"Maybe."

The next morning, Ignacio hastened to the ranch, excited to solve his mystery. As he drove through the gate, he saw two people on horses off to his left and they came galloping up to greet him. Yesenia De La Garza threw her beautiful long brown hair behind her shoulder as she slowed her white horse. Her friend, Brenda Pina trotted up behind her on a bay gelding. Ignacio smiled to see the two girls. He held high hopes that his son would somehow find favor with Yesenia. He rolled his window down. "So what are you two up to out here this morning?"

Yesenia relaxed her grip on the reins. "Just taking a ride around the ranch! It's been a while since we exercised our horses. Something's got them stirred up. I guess it's the cold wind."

"Great. But I have some traps set over there so be careful not to get in them."

"Okay! We're going the other way so it shouldn't be a problem."

"Have a good ride!"

"Bye Mr. Aguirre! See you later!"

Ignacio waved at them as they trotted away. His attention returned to his mission for the day. In his mind, he pictured finding a large mountain lion and taking pictures for the newspaper. That would keep the ranchers wanting his services. He stopped his truck a little way away from the kill and approached it with anticipation.

The trap remained just as he had left it, set and untouched. He drew closer to it, carefully avoiding touching it, to get a better look at it. A tuft of hair rested like a tease on the trap. Ignacio wanted to pick it up and look at it, but he knew better so he backed off. It almost seemed like the animal left it there to draw him into the trap. "Okay, now you're getting paranoid." No animal could lay out a trap like that.

He inspected the soil for fresh tracks and found various new ones amid the original tracks, so he knew they had been there again. "How in the hell did they not trip that trap?" Fresh tracks littered the ground inches away from his trap.

Suddenly, the sound of branches cracking came from a large thicket of brush nearby. He looked up to see what had caused it and saw nothing, so he stood up and moved closer to the brush. He expected to find a jack rabbit running away or maybe even a possum or rat. Creeping slowly towards the brush, he leaned over to get a better view through the undergrowth. Without warning, the loud scream of a large bobcat pierced his ears and sent a shiver up his spine. Instinctively, his legs shot him up and back from the bush, causing him to land unceremoniously on his rear and roll backwards.... into the trap.

The loud clunk with a simultaneous crack announced his worst fear. Racking pain shot through his body as he screamed and struggled to free his arm from the trap. He glanced back at his arm and realized, even through the gushing blood, that the trap had broken it because his wrist now bent toward his body but his elbow did not and a gleaming, white bone protruded through the skin on his forearm. Logically, he knew how to release the trap, but it took two hands and one of his hands was not working now. He screamed in anguish as he attempted to maneuver his broken arm into a position that would allow him to escape, but he simply could not do it one-handed.

A shiver crawled up his spine and he stopped moving. He turned his head towards the bush because the intense feeling of somebody watching him overwhelmed him, but he saw nothing. Turning his attention back to his trapped arm, he used his right hand to pull the trap closer to him. He stopped suddenly again and snapped his head around to face the bush. Once again, there was nothing there, so he turned back to the trap. The snap of a twig within the bush caused him to turn his head slowly towards it. The sight before him caused him to gasp. The massive bobcat standing two feet away slowly blinked his glowing eyes and yawned, flashing his enormous canines. Every time the bobcat exhaled, his breath seemed to hang visibly in the air. Now, Ignacio realized the nature of his opponent. This bobcat exceeded every size expectation known. His bulky legs sported muscles that would make a mountain lion proud.

The sudden comprehension of his dire situation caused him to panic and pull desperately at the trap to free his arm, keeping his eyes on the beast before him. Sounds of the chain striking its attached stake now blended with the low growl emanating from the bobcat. He pulled harder and faster, yanking with all of his might despite the agonizing pain of his crushed arm. Finally, he forced himself to glance away from the bobcat to the trap, hoping to find a way to release it.

Finding no possibility of release, he turned to face his attacker. To his horror, the now apparent Alpha no longer stood alone. All around him snarled bobcats of all sizes, glancing at each other in some kind of coordination. They kept their eyes on him and yawned in excitement. His eyes locked onto the eyes of the Alpha and a shiver ran up his spine, causing his ears to ring. Through the ringing, he heard a hissing voice.

"So, there you are...trapped in the trap you set for us. How does it feeeeeeeeel ssssss?"

Ignacio realized that he must be hallucinating now due to the pain. But it did not stop the vision in front of him.

The bobcats seemed to rally at the comment as they bumped into each other in solidarity. Ignacio blinked his eyes, not believing the sight. To make matters worse, he perceived that he could hear their thoughts.

"We should eat this one also."

"He carries a tooth." Ignacio knew that they were talking about his knife.

"I will bite onto it so he cannot get it with his hand. We can bring him down and eat him." The Alpha appeared to be considering the idea.

Ignacio pulled in panic against the trap once again and began to twist and turn as he kicked frantically at the bobcats. The bobcats seemed amused at his pitiful attempts to escape as they crept towards him. Suddenly, they stopped, shifting their gaze to something in the distance at the right. Ears perked in harmony, they all glanced to the Alpha who stood at a halt, listening intently to something that Ignacio could not hear. Finally in the sudden silence, he perceived the muted sound of approaching horses.

The Alpha locked eyes with Ignacio, then turned away to the increasingly louder sound of hoofs hitting the caliche as they moved closer. Ignacio struggled to make out the source of the sound. All of a sudden, two forms materialized through his blurring vision and the white outline of Yesenia's horse sharpened as it grew closer. Ignacio strained to keep his eyes on his only hope of getting out of this alive. He turned back to glance at his attackers.

They were gone.

Yesenia and Brenda rode up to Ignacio and dismounted a few feet away from Ignacio's writhing body. The horses nervously hopped around and refused to be still so Yesenia handed her reins to Brenda. She bounded over to Ignacio.

"Oh, my God! What happened to you? We heard you screaming." Yesenia winced when she saw his arm.

Ignacio shook his head. He convinced himself that he must have been hallucinating the bobcats because of the pain. "I tripped over a rock and fell into the trap," he moaned. He saw no reason to tell the girls what had really happened.

"Brenda, call Eric. He'll know how to get this trap off."

After what seemed to be an eternity to Ignacio, Eric's truck sped up to them and he jumped out. He ran to his father and released the trap, as Ignacio shrieked in agony.

"Come on, we have to get him to a hospital!" They carefully loaded Ignacio into Eric's truck.

The girls folded their arms in a shiver as they watched Eric's truck spin in the caliche and race down the road to the gate.

"Scary! How did that happen?" Yesenia doubted Ignacio's story. "I don't see how he did that. It makes no sense." The horses started jumping around again. "Let's get out of here."

They spoke little as they rode toward the horse trailer. After they loaded the horses and drove to the gate, Brenda got out of the truck to close it. Off in the distance, a bobcat screamed.

THE HOLE IN THE SKY: PORTAL ONE

CHAPTER 6

Sheriff Tim McDonald glanced toward the ringing phone next to his dispatcher, Penny Loewen, and watched as she pressed the button on her console.

"Crowder County Sheriff's Office... How can I help you?"

Tim instantly recognized the voice that came out of the speaker. Dedra Boutwell's worried tone told him that she probably had unwanted visitors again on her ranch. "This is Dedra Boutwell. Could you please tell the Sheriff that there's a bunch of illegals crossing the Sycamore towards my house? There's about fifteen of them."

Tim nodded to Penny when she turned her head towards him for a response. "I'll let him know and send someone out there as soon as possible."

"Good, because you remember the last time they came to my house, they robbed me. I won't let them come in this time."

"I understand. They're on their way."

Tim grabbed his hat off the filing cabinet. "Alert the Border Patrol."

"Yes, Sir."

Automatically checking for his side arm, he pulled his keys from his pocket and stepped out into the small parking lot to get into his car. Normally, he did not make a habit of showing up when ranchers called in illegals. The Border Patrol handled almost all

of these calls. But the Boutwells supported him at every election and he made sure to take care of them.

The five-minute drive to the ranch passed quickly and he soon pulled into the ranch. He noticed that his deputy, Shane Hill, pulled in off the highway behind him. He could always count on Shane. With no family, Shane could react quickly and be where he was needed. Dedra's house sat on the top of a hill and he saw it easily from the highway. When they drove up to it, Dedra bounded out of the door, pointing off toward the south.

"They're over there! They haven't done anything but, after last time, I'm not taking any chances."

"I don't blame you at all." Tim looked in the direction that Dedra had pointed and saw a line of men cutting through the brush with all of their gear. He noticed that the older men led the group and he thought he even recognized the leader from another arrest.

Shane tapped his arm. "Hey, ain't that old Rudolpho?" At that moment, the group leader looked up and saw Tim. He stopped in his tracks, causing his followers to bump into him from behind.

Miguel turned to Francisco. "Now what?" Then, he followed the gaze of the old man and spied the Sheriff watching them. He frowned and yelled at Rudolpho. "Are you kidding me? I thought you knew how to get us through without being seen! Now what do we do?"

"Silencio!"

The Sheriff and the old man locked eyes for a few seconds. Suddenly, Rudolpho turned and ran, dropping his load to make his escape easier. The rest of the men followed.

"Here we go." Tim and Shane took off at a sprint in the direction of the men. Dodging cactus and sagebrush, they carefully kept their eyes on the men as they headed off towards the west.

Shane pushed the button on the radio attached to his uniform. "In pursuit of ten illegals heading west."

Miguel and Francisco quickly passed up Rudolpho and the older men in their escape attempt. Rudolpho now followed them. Glancing back at their pursuers, Miguel accelerated without thinking about his course. Suddenly, a now familiar eerie, light feeling engulfed him and all the hairs on the back of his neck stood up. He took a deep breath in response and stopped. Within a few seconds, he felt the impact of Francisco's body hitting him and knocking him over. He rolled into a heap on the cold grass and realized that he must now be in the odd pasture they had so carefully avoided before. Surprisingly, a wide-eyed Rudolpho appeared abruptly, apparently forgetting his insistence on avoiding the area. Miguel stood up quickly and looked back to see the Sheriff and his deputy closing in on them.

They all looked at each other in panic. Miguel decided that he preferred going through the strange place with all of its odd sensations over taking a chance at being caught by the Sheriff. "We'll go this way. They won't follow us in here." The others nodded and they turned to continue their flight.

At first, they did not notice them. The small colored lights surrounded them and began to grow until they enveloped them completely. The men stopped again in awe. Miguel signaled to the others. "It's okay. It's okay." His confidence left him quickly, though, when the lights disappeared within a blink. He turned to continue on his path but he suddenly realized that he could not breathe. Struggling to suck oxygen in with his lungs, he noticed that something black and smoky now blanketed him and it stung as it filled his lungs with something that smelled like sulfur. His lungs responded with violent coughs that threw his body all around. Then, he saw them. Red, glowing eyes formed immediately in front of him and he panicked. He saw the others in the same grip of death. He had to get away.

With his last burst of energy, he forced his legs to carry him back out of the area. When he reached the edge of the pasture, his lungs once again filled with air and he bent over, sucking it in as hard as he could between coughs. Francisco and the others came tumbling out with him in the same condition. Concentrating on the act of breathing, they did not care that the Sheriff and the deputy now closed in on them.

Tim watched in confusion as the men he was chasing suddenly appeared in front of him, all coughing and sputtering. Shane caught up to him.

"What the hell happened to them?"

"Don't know but let's get them rounded up."

The Border Patrol drove up and began to process the ashen men. Miguel pointed into the pasture and gasped, "Malo, malo, malo!"

Shane tapped Tim on the shoulder. "What's bad? Do you smell sulphur? Did you see anything?"

"Yeah, I smell it. I didn't see anything but it really got 'em whatever it was!" Tim shrugged and walked towards his car slowly, trying not to think about it. It did not work.

A sudden chill ran up his spine and he stopped to look back.

CHAPTER 7

David Sergeant Jr. dropped the wrench from his hand with a thud and reached back for his water jug. After taking a swig, he wiped his mouth on his sleeve and inspected his work. Pride filled him as he looked over the third successful well he had finished for his new customer, Reverend William Harris. Still, he had to wonder. As he drove home, he thought more about his newest customer.

The Reverend had purchased this land only a year ago from another rancher who had finally given up trying to run it because it had no water on it. David tried several times to dig a good well for the previous owner but never could locate any water. Obviously, something had changed. But how? Maybe it had something to do with the small fault lines that had formed since he had been there before. Several of these had also occurred on various other ranches. Talk of the town people indicated that it must have something to do with fracking.

David's first meeting with the Reverend and his aide had caused him to wonder even then. David arrived at the ranch a few minutes before the black Escalade with its darkened windows pulled up. The driver door opened, revealing a tall, thin young man in new blue jeans who stepped out onto the caliche with his perfect boots. He lifted his Oakley sunglasses and gave David a friendly, but guarded, smile. Then he stepped forward to the passenger door and opened it.

David did not know what he had expected of the famous Reverend William Harris, but the person who emerged from the car took him by surprise. The older, slightly disheveled man standing before him reminded him of a very fat wino. His eyes looked empty and the pungent smell of someone who had skipped a few baths assaulted his nose. David gave the aide a curious glance, but the aide shook his head and looked off to one side. This man bore no resemblance to the great preacher he had watched a couple of years ago on TV as he staunchly carried his Bible and delivered an outstanding sermon to his enormous Church in San Antonio.

David stepped forward. "Hi. David Sergeant, Jr. Nice to meet you, Sir." He offered his hand to the Reverend.

The Reverend frowned and backed off slightly. He gave David a slight nod, leaving him standing there with his arm awkwardly extended so he dropped it to his side. A gruff voice arose from the reverend. "You dig wells?"

"Yes, Sir."

"I need at least three wells."

"Where would you like me to put them?" David tried to hide the lack of confidence he held for the project.

"Dan will show you." Then the old man turned and walked off abruptly, leaving David standing there.

The aide took his cue and gave David a proper handshake. "Hi. I'm Dan Reynolds. I can show you where he wants the wells."

"Where's he going?" David followed the Reverend with his eyes as the old man seemingly wandered off to nowhere.

Dan took a deep breath. "I never know. He wanders all over the ranch lately." He turned and watched the Reverend disappear over the hill.

David took off his hat and cocked his head slightly. "Is he always like that?'

"No, I mean yes. I mean he wasn't, but now he is." He frowned. "To be honest, I'm very worried about him. I think he's got Alzheimer's or something. This is not the man I hired on with."

"I was going to ask you about that. I watched him on TV a couple of years ago and he's really changed, even his voice."

Dan's face dropped. "Yeah, I know." He turned to look at David. "All of this started a year ago when we came out to go hunting on his lease. He went out on the first morning, but when he came back, he was not the same man."

"What do you mean?"

"When he left hunting camp, he was joking around and being his usual self. When he came back, he wasn't laughing about anything. We all thought he was just coming down with something so we wanted to load up and go home. He refused to go. Then, he spent the whole rest of the week wandering around the ranch. He begrudgingly came home with us and we thought that he would come around after he got some sleep."

"Was he sick?"

Dan shook his head. "If that was the problem, he's still sick and getting worse. He never ran fever or anything like that. But his whole attitude soured. The normally jovial man we had worked with for years began to complain about everyone around him and he shunned us when we tried to talk to him about it. He got so angry with me one day that he yelled obscenities all down the hallway of our office building."

"Really? What made him so mad?"

Dan shook his head. "I brought him his coffee and it wasn't hot enough."

"Wow."

"But the yelling wasn't the worst of it. He started taking the Church's money."

"You're kidding!"

"I wish I was. He had me call all around out here to find out if the ranch next to this one was for sale."

"You mean the Boutwell ranch?"

"Yeah. When he found out that the Boutwell family didn't have it for sale, he tried to offer them three times the price per acre of the most expensive ranch around here. They refused to sell. I thought he was going to have a heart attack over that. Then, he wanted to know about this ranch. When he offered the owner the same deal as he had offered the Boutwell family, the guy sold it to him in a heartbeat. I tried to tell him that I had researched the property and that there was no water, but he didn't seem to care. He was determined to buy it."

David frowned. "And now he thinks I can find water?"

"He's positive. But that wasn't the worst of it."

"What else?"

Dan looked down at his hands. "I thought he was going to buy it with his own money. Goodness knows he has plenty of money of his own to buy the ranch. But he wrote a check out of the Church account for the place."

"Really? Wow. That takes a lot of gall."

"Yeah, the Deacons called him in to a meeting immediately after the bank statement came in. You would think that he would be worried about it, but as the meeting time came closer, he grew more and more upbeat."

"About what?"

"Who knows? All I know is that he looked almost maniacal when he marched into the room. He did not even let them ask him about the money. He just strode into the room and announced that he had made all of the money for the Church and that he would spend it as he pleased. Then, he turned and left the room, slamming the door behind him."

"Incredible. And he's not in jail?"

"The Deacons are still arguing about what to do about it. In the meantime, here we are."

"So what do I do? Just go ahead and dig the wells?"

"What would it hurt to try? Besides, do you want to be the one who tells him no?"

David raised his eyebrows and stared off in the direction the old man took. Then he turned back to face Dan. "So, where do you want me to put the first one?"

THE HOLE IN THE SKY: PORTAL ONE

CHAPTER 8

Dana threw her briefcase into the back seat of her red Focus and closed the back door. She glanced up to the windows of her classroom to make sure she had turned off the lights, then got into her car and started the engine. Driving on the street in front of the school, she watched her students as they loaded into their cars to go home for the day. Noticing Harmony sliding into Ricky's passenger seat, she shook her head. When would teen-aged girls figure out that they could not depend on their boyfriends? Harmony showed such potential but Ricky would hold her back. She needed to be stronger than that.

She turned onto the street that would take her home and switched on the music to distract her from those thoughts. Just ahead, she saw Dwayne, one of the 'Watchers', standing two feet away from the road. "I guess it's Dwayne's turn today."

She frowned. Dwayne usually watched everyone driving down his stretch of the street and waved and smiled, but he was apparently continuing the unusual behavior he showed her earlier in the day. He stood transfixed, staring up at the sky to the west. Dana followed his gaze and saw the object of his gawk, that peculiar hole in the sky.

Dana had first noticed this strange aberration in the sky a couple of years ago during a rainy spell. The low, dark clouds dominated the sky that day as the heavy rain fell everywhere, but she sighted an odd area just above the ranch that belonged to her teacher friend, Dedra Boutwell. Positioned in the middle of the storm clouds, the gap absolutely glowed with sunshine; beams of light leading all the way to the pasture below. The clearing persisted for three days in a row. Further, when the stormy clouds cleared away everywhere else with the passing of the cold front, the odd gap became filled with a huge, dark cloud. Dana observed it every day for several weeks and realized that the aperture did exactly the opposite of whatever surrounded it.

So, today, when Dana saw Dwayne's peculiar gaze, she began to wonder. "That's odd. I'm going to have to ask Dedra about that pasture."

She turned off the highway onto the narrow road that led to her walking path along the creek. Parking her car, she stepped out and put on her walking shoes. Then she placed her visor on her head and began to stretch. She glanced at her watch and began a quick walk along the path, breathing deeply to take in the fresh air after being in her classroom all day. Her walk almost always lifted her spirits, but her headache began to throb as she made her way down the path. She decided to walk through it. Maybe it would go away in a few minutes.

She stepped up the pace and carefully avoided the muddy spots along the path. And she noticed several large cracks in her path that had never been there before. Her headache began to improve and she took a deep breath, following the path as it curved sharply to the right. She stopped to catch her breath and closed her eyes and bent over, leaning on her knees. Suddenly, a chill ran up her spine and she quickly stood up and looked around. An odd sound compelled her to look up into the tall trees at the edge of the creek. She gasped and stepped back.

The sight before her freaked her out. Jagged, dead tree trunks jutted out from the dark water, branching with bare limbs in all directions. That alone did not bother her as she had seen it many times on her walks. But today was different. Resting on the lifeless branches, at least twenty huge, black vultures scrutinized her with their black piercing eyes. The smell of stagnant water insulted her sense of smell. She had never seen anything like this before. She blinked, hoping that they would disappear, but they maintained their evil glare on her. She thought she saw something black slide behind one of the trees. She felt something crawling up her leg so she looked down to find a scorpion and quickly flicked it off. When she looked back down, she gasped as she saw a group of at least a dozen scorpions on the trail. She had to get away from there so she began to back away slowly down the path. When she got around the curve, she turned around and began sprinting along the path on her way quickly to her car. Resting beside her tire, two snakes began to hiss at her. She fumbled for her keys and hastily opened the door to jump into the car and lock the door behind her. *What is happening here? I have never seen scorpions or snakes on this trail before.*

Remembering that Dedra was a bird watcher, she shuddered. "I'm going to have to ask Dedra about vultures too."

Dedra pulled her chair across the porch to position it in a place that would allow her to view the panorama across the pasture in front of her house. Then she sat down and picked up the binoculars hanging from her neck. She took a deep breath. She loved moments like these when she could relax and do some bird watching. With the temperatures cooling, many of the birds would be flying south so she might be able to spy some species that did not normally live in her area of Texas. She focused the binoculars to see the tree line on the other side of the pasture. At first, she found only various sparrows, but as she spanned the tree line she noticed a cardinal and then a Ladder Back Woodpecker. Smiling at her finds, she continued to search, hoping to spy a warbler or two.

She shivered a bit as the sun began to set. Knowing that the visibility was too low now to watch the birds, she dropped her binoculars and started to stand up. But as she did, she stopped suddenly when she noticed the lights dancing around in the pasture.

These lights reminded her of the famous Marfa Lights that supposedly fly randomly around in the desert close to Marfa. People came to Marfa from many miles away to sit on their vehicles and watch the odd, colored lights dash through the air. Experts of every kind attempted to explain the Marfa Lights, but nobody had actually proven any of the theories projected. The speculations ranged from something like the Northern Lights to alien crafts zooming over the land or even ghosts.

Dedra did not know exactly what they were but she knew that they loved her pasture. On almost any given evening, the lights silently zipped through the night air, varying in intensity, color and size as they followed what seemed to be random paths and danced around each other. She had lost her initial fear of them long ago after realizing that they never seemed to do any harm. Still, she had to wonder. And tonight, the lights dashed around with seemingly extraordinary energy.

With all of the activity of the Sheriff's chase, the day had already unnerved her some. The frantic look on the faces of the men who were arrested made her wonder what they had seen. The fact that they had turned around in the middle of the chase and run to the Sheriff and his deputy to beg to be arrested confounded her. What had they seen? She knew they had ventured into that odd pasture.

The realization that none of her livestock would venture into the pasture told her that something must be different there. Did it have anything to do with the lights? Normally, her horses would strive to get into an area covered with grass like that. But the horses avoided the pasture, even walking the entire distance around it to sidestep it. Odd.

The guesthouse at the edge of the pasture caught her attention. Her daughters planned to have their slumber party in the little house this weekend and they had been cleaning it to get it ready. Most of the time, the lodge served as her studio where she carved birds from wood and painted them, but all of her supplies had been moved to accommodate the party. Still, that did not explain all of the odd things that had been going on in the house before the cleaning began.

Usually, the girls ignored the house and they had not been in it until they started cleaning it yesterday. But somebody must have been in there in the last few weeks. The last time she went in it, she noticed that all of her brushes had been moved from their normal places. Maybe it had something to do with the frog.

She kept the brushes she was using in a big glass jar with water and they were so crowded together that she was forced to struggle to remove one to use it. She had been painting for several hours when all of the brushes exploded out of the jar suddenly. She stared in confusion at the now empty jar as a huge frog rose up from the water and gazed at her, making a loud vibrating croak. It hopped out of the jar and made its way to the open door toward the pasture as she watched it with her mouth agape.

It made no sense. She had pushed several different brushes into that water and they had gone all the way down to the bottom of the jar. The frog was so big that it filled the jar completely. So how had any of the brushes fit into the jar at all? She shook her head at the thought.

Still, she hoped that the girls could enjoy themselves this weekend.

THE HOLE IN THE SKY: PORTAL ONE

CHAPTER 9

Luke turned away from the counter of the Burger Place as Debbie Cortes pulled a foam cup off the top of a tall stack and began filling it with black coffee. He scanned the tables in the small room to see where he would like to sit. As usual, Tim and David hovered over their coffee cups at the table in the middle of the room.

Luke picked up his coffee. "Thank ya, Debbie."

"Sure, Luke."

He set his cup down when he got to the table and seated himself for his mid-morning meeting with all of the town's most important people. One of the chairs lacked its usual occupant. "Where's Ignacio?"

Tim scooted his chair out a bit. "He'll be here any minute. He's moving a little slower since he broke his arm. At least, that's his excuse."

David scratched his head. "Now, tell me again how that happened. I got some story about him tripping and falling into a trap."

Tim shrugged. "That's what he said. Didn't say any more than that."

"Hmm. I can't imagine that. That's some bad luck." Luke shook his head. "I heard you had a good catch yesterday, Tim."

"Yep. Those illegals just turned themselves in. Makes my job a lot easier." He paused as he remembered the chill he felt in the day's events, and then he shook it off and looked back at Luke. "What you been up to Luke?"

"Aw, just the usual." Luke swallowed hard and refused to think about the events of the past few days. Admitting what he had thought he saw would open him up to some powerful ridicule. He nonchalantly looked away until his eyes caught a view of the new deep scratches on his truck. He blinked and quickly looked back to the table.

They all stopped talking and watched as a green Ford pickup pulled into the parking lot and Ignacio stepped out slowly. The cast on his arm rested in a blue sling so he grabbed his cap with his good arm and closed the truck door.

"See? I told you. He's just slower now." Tim squinted his eyes as he watched Ignacio open the door and walk in. "I think he's on drugs," he said loudly.

Ignacio reacted. "Only the best!" He walked to the table and set his cap down.

"The usual please, Debbie."

Debbie looked back to the kitchen. Casey Tipps nodded and started Ignacio's breakfast taco without any further instruction. Debbie poured his coffee and took it out to him.

She gave Ignacio a concerned look. "What happened to you? You haven't been here in a couple of days and now you come in here with that cast."

Ignacio shrugged. "Uhmm. It's a long story." He shuddered inwardly and did his best to hide it from the others.

Debbie put her hands on her hips. "You're gonna have to give me more than that. How can I worry about you if I don't know what happened?"

Tim laughed. "I know you think you're our momma just because you cook our breakfast every day, but Ignacio doesn't have to answer to you if he doesn't want to."

Debbie took her hands off her hips and bent down to give Ignacio a small kiss on the cheek. "Tell momma what happened." She cocked her head and smiled.

Ignacio grinned through his now blushing face. "Oh, okay. I fell into one of my traps and it broke my arm. Happy?"

Debbie frowned. "No. I want you to be more careful. Do you hear me?"

"Yes, mommy."

Debbie gave him a look. "That's better."

They all laughed as she turned and walked back behind the counter. David stopped laughing as he looked out one of the many large glass windows that encircled them. He tapped Luke and indicated that he should look out the window. Luke followed his gaze and noticed the black Escalade pulling into the parking lot. The others did the same and watched as Dan jumped out and opened the door for the Reverend.

Tim broke the silence. "Who *is* that? I've seen them around a couple of times."

David shook his head. "That, Tim, is the Reverend William Harris and his aide Dan Reynolds. I just finished digging three wells on the old Williams ranch for them. Reverend Harris bought it last year. He's also looking to buy the south side of the Simpson ranch."

"Oh, I remember seeing him on TV once. Now, what in the hell would a preacher want with a ranch?"

"Yeah, they're different. Dan is okay, but that Reverend is crazy."

The conversation ended as Dan and the Reverend opened the door and walked in.

Reverend Harris stepped up to the counter and read the menu hanging above him as he rubbed his large belly. He turned to Dan. "Get me two egg and cheese burritos and a large coffee." He turned away from the counter and headed to the restroom.

Dan Reynolds smiled nervously at Debbie and ordered their breakfast as he searched in the back pocket of his slacks for his money clip. He pulled out a twenty and handed it to her. Then, he checked the room quickly to find a suitable location for his boss to sit. He saw David and gave him a small wave before he went to a table across the room as soon as the drinks were ready. The Reverend came out of the restroom just in time for Debbie to deliver their breakfast.

Dan watched as the Reverend tore into his burritos, barely taking a breath between bites. The Reverend's eating habits had changed drastically, along with all of his other habits. Instead of eating fruits and healthy food, the Reverend now consumed copious amounts of high-fat foods and sweets. He constantly called for his staff to bring him candy, chips and colas through the days he spent at the office. And he insisted on going to expensive restaurants for lunch, paying for his feasts with more of the Church money.

The Reverend had also adopted a new work ethic. He began to get to work later and later until he rarely made it to his office before afternoon. The only morning he worked was Sunday morning and that was because he had to preach. His sermons now left his parishioners confused and discomforted. When the Deacons asked him about it, he told them he did not care. The people needed to know the truth about the real power in the world. Obviously, something spiritual had happened.

Later in the day, Debbie and Casey wiped the tables and carefully straightened up all the chairs after all the customers left. Then Debbie remembered that she needed to talk to Casey about something.

"Hey, Casey. Did you lock the door last night when you left?

"Yes. Why?"

"Because it was unlocked when I came in this morning."

"What? That's impossible! I locked it just like I always lock it."

"And whoever came in here pulled hamburger meat out of the refrigerator and drug it around all over the floor in the kitchen. I had to clean it all up before I could get the breakfast run started."

"You're kidding! Who would have a key? Who would do something like that?"

"Dunno. Just be careful to make sure the door is locked. Okay?"

"Sure."

Debbie grabbed her purse and headed out the door, leaving Casey to finish up. When she got home she pulled a small bag out of her purse.

"Come on, my babies. Momma brought you a treat."

Five cats appeared from nowhere, rubbing her ankles and purring as she bent over to scoop out meat and cheese scraps she had saved for them. She lovingly scratched their ears and stroked their fur.

"That's my good babies."

THE HOLE IN THE SKY: PORTAL ONE

CHAPTER 10

Dana pulled her car into her parking place at the back of the school. She had set her alarm to wake her at an earlier time for this morning so she could visit with Dedra. The events of the previous day with the Watchers and the vultures had unnerved her a bit and she had slept fitfully. The feeling that something was wrong tugged at her mind and that feeling kept growing stronger.

She unlocked the back door to the school and quickly opened the door to her classroom to slide her briefcase under her desk. Then she walked briskly around the corner to get to Dedra's room. After knocking on the door she announced, "It's me!"

Dedra's voice responded, "Come on in!"

Dana pulled the door closed behind her. "Hey. I had a couple of questions I needed to ask you. Do you have a moment?"

"Yeah, sure. What do you want to know?'

Dana paused because she wondered just how she could ask Dedra these questions without appearing to be crazy. Then she decided that Dedra must already think she was crazy so she just blurted out the first question. "I was running along the creek yesterday and I found these dead trees with huge vultures sitting on them. I mean, there had to be at least forty of them just sitting there staring at me. I don't remember ever seeing them there before. I know you watch birds. Is it normal for them to be here at this time of the year?"

Dedra smiled. "It depends on what kind of vultures they are. If they are the Black-headed Vultures, yes. They always spend the winter around here. But I didn't think they liked to be anywhere that people go regularly. I bet that was a sight."

"Yes. They just sat there staring. They were pretty ugly."

"Was there something dead around there? Maybe they were planning on having a feast on something there."

"I didn't see anything or smell anything."

"Maybe they decided that they liked that place for a roost."

Dana nodded. "That must be it. I just hadn't ever seen them there before."

"Okay. That was easy. You said a couple of questions. What else?"

"I never asked you this before but I always wanted to. You know I drive past your ranch every day."

"Yeah?"

"Well I noticed something odd and I wondered if you had ever noticed it."

Dedra frowned. "Like what?"

"I know you'll probably think I don't have enough to think about to notice this, but there's a place over your ranch that seems to be different from any other place there. I mean, when the rest of the sky is covered with clouds, it's clear and has sunbeams coming out of it. When the rest of the sky is clear, it's cloudy there. Have you ever noticed it?"

Dedra paused as she looked at Dana. "I thought I was the only one who noticed that. And that's not the only weird thing about that pasture."

"Really?" Dana did not even try to hide her enthusiasm. "What else makes it weird?"

"Where do I begin? The horses and goats won't go in there, even though it's the best grass on the whole ranch. The weirdest thing is the lights."

"Lights?"

"Oh yeah. They're like the Marfa Lights."

"Oh, I know about those! Wow! But they don't know what causes those. What do your lights look like?"

"They're small and bright and have different colors. They fly around all over the pasture and never anywhere else."

"Wow. Haven't you ever wondered what they are?"

"Well, sure. But they never hurt anyone or anything. The UPS man is terrified of them though." She laughed. "I've finally accepted them and I actually like to watch them. Just part of living on this ranch. Why don't you come see them sometime?"

"I'd like that. Let me know when they show up again."

"Sure. Anything else?"

Dana thought about mentioning the scorpions and snakes but decided against it. "No,

I guess I'd better get over to my classroom and get ready for the day. Thanks!"

"Sure. Anytime."

Dana walked quickly down the hall, happy to know that she was not crazy. So, something strange was truly going on there. She could hardly wait until she could see the lights. She rounded the corner and nearly ran into Savannah, Heather and April as they huddled giggling in the hallway about their adventures in mudding. "What is so funny, girls?"

The trio ducked their heads and busted out laughing. April looked up. "Oh, nothing!"

Dana shook her head. At least somebody was in a good mood today. Maybe today would be better than yesterday. That would not be hard. She opened the door and the three girls walked in, followed by the rest of her First Period students. Dana got the class settled in and began her lesson for the day.

The lesson involved a discussion about logic. The students, who had heard lectures on logic too many times in the past, began to grimace at the thought of hearing it all again. But Dana surprised them.

"Today, I want to talk about one of the most frequent errors in logic. Can anyone tell me what they think it might be?" The students looked at her and shook their heads, but they seemed relieved that this lecture was not the same one they could repeat in their sleep. "Is it possible to prove that something cannot exist?"

Heather raised her hand. "What do you mean?"

"Can you prove that something does not exist?" She looked around the room. The faces looking up at her told her that they did not know the answer. "For example, can we prove that Bigfoot does not exist?" Immediately, the students reacted. "What do you think?"

Savannah raised her hand. "I think they do exist. I mean, there have been too many sightings by too many people and they have found tracks."

"But scientists say that Bigfoot does not exist because they have no proof."

Raymond raised his hand. "Try telling that to those people who have seen him!"

Dana smiled. "Exactly. When someone sees something like that, they know what they've seen. But they don't have any proof. Does that mean it doesn't exist?"

Raymond practically jumped out of his chair. "No!"

"Scientists have become very sloppy about saying things cannot exist, simply because they have no proof. It's true that you cannot say it does exist, but you also cannot say it does not exist. Can anyone think of some things that they said didn't exist and then later had to admit that they were wrong?"

April raised her hand. "Air."

"That's right! For centuries, scientists had no proof that air existed, yet it obviously did. Just because we, as humans, didn't have the equipment to prove the presence of air, it did not mean that air didn't exist. Yet, we make the same error today. Can anyone think of some other things like that?"

Amy raised her hand. "Bacteria."

"Right! Bacteria killed millions of people before we could prove their existence. Another example happened in the 1800's. Wealthy people went on safari in Africa and came back ranting about a hairy ape-man. The rigid scientific community at the time denounced these people, saying that if such a creature existed, they would have a skeleton. Well, now you can go to any zoo and see...a gorilla. Have you heard the 'we don't have a skeleton' argument about anything else?" The students all nodded. Dana paused and looked around the room. "What about other things? Are there any things that you know of that could not be explained by science with proof?"

Jason raised his hand. "Ghosts? Aliens? Nessie?"

"Yes, there are plenty of things that people swear they see or experience and yet, they have no proof. Even though it would be great if there was proof, it is an error in logic to declare that they don't exist. Do you know of any other strange things that may have no proof?"

April looked at Savannah and Heather and shrugged her shoulders. "Why not?"

"April?"

"We saw some very strange coyotes yesterday. They were not normal. They had glowing eyes and they were huge. They were trying to kill Genie Nixon's goats."

Dana got a chill as she heard what April said. She lived close to Genie. "Wow. Really?"

"We had to fight them off with pepper spray."

The rest of the class half-giggled. Dana kept her eyes on April. Why would she make up something like that? "Now class, don't laugh. What if it happened to you and you had no proof? You know what you saw, but nobody believes you just because there is no physical proof."

THE HOLE IN THE SKY: PORTAL ONE

"Just go ask Genie!" April's face reddened. The class silenced. April held the respect of all of her peers.

"Savannah and I were there too! We saw it." Heather spoke up to defend her friend.

Dana decided she needed to change the direction of the discussion away from the girls. "Anyone else have a strange event around here?"

Ashley raised her hand. "My bedroom door slammed shut by itself last night and everybody else in the house was asleep. I think it was a ghost." She looked around at all her friends staring at her. "And ask J.J. about the glass that threw itself across his kitchen yesterday."

J.J.'s mouth dropped open as he realized that he had just been thrown into the conversation. He gave a weak smile. "Uhm, yeah. It did."

Dana tried to hide the chill that kept crawling up her spine as she listened to the stories of her students. "You see? Things like this happen. And we must keep an open mind."

As if on cue, the door to the chemical storeroom swung open. Dana's mind began to see things in slow motion. For a second, she believed she had a ghost in her own classroom. Then, she saw it. A squirrel came bounding around the corner after it hit the door open, scrambling toward the desks. The students shrieked in horror and leaped out of their chairs. To Dana, it looked like they were doing "the wave" like at a football game. The whole scene looked comical...until the squirrel turned and raced towards her. She found herself shrieking like her students and jumping up on her desk. All the students danced on their desks as they screamed. Finally, the squirrel ran back into the chemical closet. Dana climbed down off her sanctuary and ran to the closet door to slam it closed. She turned around.

"It's okay now. You can get off the desks. It's locked in the closet." One by one, the students cautiously came down off the desks. She called the custodians and they gingerly opened the door to the closet. The squirrel lay dead on the floor. A ceiling tile in the closet was pushed aside.

The custodians explained what they had seen. "We think the squirrel got into the attic somehow and came down through the moved ceiling tile. Who knows? Anyway, it's dead now."

After the custodians had hauled the limp body of the squirrel out of the room, Dana got the class seated again. "And then, sometimes there are other explanations for the things we see." The class laughed as the bell rang.

Dana locked the door after the last of her class walked out. After the events of that class, she welcomed her conference period for a chance to rethink what had just occurred and what her students were telling her. The tension in the building continued to pull at her attention. She shivered. Wrapping her arms around herself, she shook her head. What was going on around here?

She turned to go to her desk and get some paperwork done. Suddenly, she did not feel alone. She stopped abruptly and inhaled deeply. When she exhaled, she saw her breath and frowned. The temperature in the room must have plummeted for some reason and she swung around to go have a look at the thermostat. Then, she saw it and gasped. The black shadow, standing only a few feet away from her, hovered slightly off the ground. It slowly began to move toward her and she instinctively began to back away from it. She closed her eyes.

"Jesus save me!"

Before she even opened her eyes, she knew that it was gone. Shaking violently, she stood there for a few seconds staring at the location where she had seen the apparition. Then, she grabbed her chair and sat down, leaning her head on the arm resting on her desk. What just happened?

The thoughts raced through her head. She must be crazy! Or, the stories of her students must have set her up for that hallucination. That must be it. That and her meeting with Dedra this morning planted the idea in her head. She picked up her head and nodded it quickly.

THE HOLE IN THE SKY: PORTAL ONE

"I am simply going to have to get more sleep!"

Only, she knew she would not be able to sleep after seeing what she had just seen.

CHAPTER 11

Ignacio shifted in his chair at the small table in the Burger Place in an attempt to relieve some of the pain radiating from his arm. The pain meds were good, but they only took an edge off his pain. He gave a slight grimace and tried to keep a pleasant look on his face as Tim rambled on about the arrest he had made earlier in the morning.

"I'm tellin you. The crazies are coming out of the woods this week! I've never been on a domestic dispute call like that! The idiot turned on me with that knife and I had to draw on him. He's lucky he's alive. If he hadn't tripped over that small fault, I would have been forced to shoot him."

David set his coffee cup down. "Yeah, I saw the ambulance heading towards you. I'm glad it was him not you with that knife stuck in the chest."

"He fell on it just right. Anymore to the left, and it would have hit his heart."

"Was he drunk?"

"No. That was the strange thing. He was doing all that on pure air. But, he's always been a little that way. His wife said she didn't know what got into him. He has never tried to attack her before."

The sound of a song playing erupted from Ignacio's pocket. He reached with his good arm and pulled it out, pushing the button to answer it. "Hello."

The voice on the phone could be heard by everyone at the table. "Ignacio! I need you out here pronto! Those damned bobcats have struck again."

"Hold on." Ignacio's face paled a bit at the sound of Billy's voice. He rolled his eyes and struggled to get out of his chair to take the call outside. He did not want his buddies to hear anything Billy might say. He stepped outside the door to continue the conversation. "Now, what happened?"

"They killed another steer! I know you're laid up with that arm, but I hope you can come out here and tell me what to do. This has got to stop!"

"I'm sorry to hear that, Billy." Billy had no idea how really very sorry he was to hear that. The thought of going out to that ranch again caused his heart to race. "I tried all the traps I have. I really don't know what else to do." At this point, he did not care if Billy thought he was incompetent.

"Don't tell me that! There's got to be somebody you know that can get this stopped. I pay a lot of money to that trapper organization of yours. You've got to do something, man."

Ignacio knew he was right. He took a deep breath and expelled it quickly. "Okay. I'll see what I can do. Where is the kill?"

"It's right over there where the other one was. There's got to be some kind of nest of them over there."

Ignacio hated how close to the truth Billy's statement came. "Yeah. I'll get out there."

"Thanks Ignacio. I appreciate it."

Billy had no idea how sick his words made Ignacio feel. His attempts to convince himself that all of the nightmares he had been having about that situation had failed miserably. He kept telling himself that it was all a hallucination, but something inside him kept screaming back against that logic. He was terrified.

THE HOLE IN THE SKY: PORTAL ONE

Ignacio opened the door to the café and waved at his friends. "Gotta go check this out. See you tomorrow." He walked to his truck and carefully climbed in. There was no way he was going out there alone. Not this time. He pressed a picture on his phone and listened while it dialed.

"Hey, Dad! What're you up to?"

"Eric, I'm going to have to get back out to that ranch with the bobcats. Will you go with me?"

Eric frowned. His Dad concerned him. Eric had never known him to be like this. "Sure Dad. Come pick me up."

Ignacio took a deep breath. At least he would not be alone out there. He drove to his house and loaded up his favorite big guns. He would be ready this time. Then, he drove to Eric's house to pick him up.

Dan turned the Escalade into the entrance of the Reverend's ranch. He glanced over at his passenger to see if there had been any change in his demeanor. He took a deep breath and opened the door to get out and open the gate. The last light of the sun quickly disappeared behind the horizon and the chill of the night caused him to zip his coat before climbing back into the Escalade. The Reverend never even blinked as Dan slid behind the wheel.

The same routine repeated itself every day. The Reverend ate his massive supper at the café and then turned to Dan. "Take me to the RV." The Reverend said the same words in exactly the same tone every day. The silence in the Escalade quickly enveloped them as they drove to the ranch. Then, Dan would drive to the RV and the Reverend would get out and go into the RV.

So, once again, Dan delivered the Reverend to his RV. He shook his head as he turned the Escalade around to leave. A chill came up his spine. Why did it always seem so dark here?

The Reverend had not gone home for several months now. Dan knew that the old man was surely losing it. His behavior increasingly deteriorated from bad to something else...evil? The empty glares that the Reverend held on him gripped him in a kind of fear that he had never experienced before. Dan feared looking back at him because the old man's eyes were vacant. There was nothing there. It reminded him of looking into a dark closet or the eyes of a goat. Or maybe it was like both. The Reverend's phone rang constantly, but he never even reacted to it anymore. The Reverend had just checked out or something. It was the 'or something' that worried Dan the most.

As Dan drove away from the RV once again, he glanced into the rear-view mirror. A flash of light caught his attention and he stopped to keep an eye on the RV. The lights in the RV began to flicker violently. Then they all went black. Dan stared at the scene in the mirror for a few seconds before he decided to go on back to his hotel room.

The next morning, he drove back to the ranch, knowing exactly what he would find. He quietly knocked on the door of the RV and waited for a response. After a few moments, the door opened a couple of inches and he jumped back when a scorpion dropped to the ground from the doorway. He waited to see if the Reverend would welcome him to come in, but silence followed the opening of the door again. So he peeked into the dark RV, half expecting some wild animal to charge him from in there. After all, it did look like a dark cave. And his expectation was not too far from the truth.

The Reverend sat on a chair, glaring at him.

"Reverend Harris? Are you okay?" He waited for a response but there was none, as usual. The picture before him was the same as it had been every day for the last month. Dirt and plant matter attached to the Reverend's hair randomly dropped off of him as he breathed. Rips and shredded pieces of cloth covered his shirt and pants and, once again, the Reverend had shed his socks and shoes before obviously running around the ranch. Dirt and mud caked his feet and a thorn perched on the side of his foot, completely unnoticed. Had he been wrestling a bear?

Dan shook his head. "Come on Reverend. Let's get you cleaned up so you can go to breakfast."

The mention of food snapped the Reverend out of his trance. "Oh, yeah."

Dan retrieved some clean clothes from the tiny closet while the Reverend stepped into the bathroom and took a quick shower. Dan handed him his clothes and he dressed wordlessly before he walked out of the RV and seated himself in the Escalade. Dan realized that food, and plenty of it, served as the Reverend's only connection with reality. And he wondered how long that would last. If the Reverend ever stopped eating, Dan would be forced to take him to a hospital. He knew that he probably should anyway, but he actually feared the Reverend's reaction.

THE HOLE IN THE SKY: PORTAL ONE

CHAPTER 12

Dana loved her weekends, normally. But normal failed to describe anything in Dana's life right now. The events of her Friday morning class foreshadowed her entire weekend and colored her mood considerably. Friday evenings used to be a signal that she could relax, but this Friday evening signaled something else.

To make matters worse, Lola failed to answer any of her calls as she tried to figure out where she was. Dana knew that her daughter was probably just running with those delinquents again. She seriously considered calling the sheriff for help finding her, but she reconsidered when she realized that she would not know what to say. She could just hear herself. "I am a terrible mother and I do not know where my daughter is. Can you help me find her?"

She knew that her husband would be able to find her. He had left Dana for the other woman. Heaven knows he thought just like his daughter.

This single parent thing left her weak and ineffective. She could handle a class full of teenagers, but when it came to her own teenager, she was clueless as to how to rein her in.

So she resorted to pacing for a while until she got tired. She would just have to wait until Lola came home and have it out with her again. She turned the TV on and sat in front of it, staring at it with her eyes glazed over until she dropped into a fitful sleep. The sound of her dogs barking pulled her out of her sleep and she sat up looking around into the darkness. For some reason, the TV showed only static and all of the lights in the house had gone out. Confusion surrounded her like the darkness. Then, she saw it.

A blackness that was darker than the darkness of the room floated above the TV. Dana struggled to stand up and tripped over the shoe she had kicked off earlier in an effort to back away from it. "Oh, no. Not again." She backed up until she reached the desk in the dining area of the room and then fumbled in the drawer, grabbing a flashlight. Without taking her eyes off the black mist, she pointed the flashlight toward it and turned it on. The very second she flipped the flashlight on, all the lights in the house turned back on and the TV cleared. She stood there shaking in the middle of the room, staring at....nothing. She blinked and rubbed her eyes.

The sound of a car approaching on the caliche of the drive made her look out the front window. Sure enough, Lola was finally home. Now, anger replaced Dana's fear. Lola opened the door.

"Where have you been and why didn't you answer my calls?"

"Whoa, Mom. I was at play practice and we had to turn our phones off."

Dana looked at the clock. "Until one-thirty in the morning?"

"Oh, uh, then we all went to the Red Bridge."

"And I suppose you were all drinking sodas, right?"

Lola raised her eyebrow. "Uh, yeah."

Dana walked up close to her daughter and took an audible sniff. "Well what did you add to that soda? It smells a lot like beer."

Lola pushed away from her mother and yelled. "Yeah. And what about it? I got home okay!"

"Don't you yell at me, young lady! I was worried sick about you." Dana began to choke up. "And I'm the only one who worries about you! But you don't give a damn that I'm home pacing the floor over you! I don't know why I bother. You are determined to do yourself in...maybe I should just let you do it." She broke down in sobs.

Lola exhaled and looked at her mother. "Mom. I'm sorry, but you can't keep thinking that I am a little girl. I didn't do anything tonight that every other teenager in the world does."

"But you are not just any teenager. You are MY teenager and I care about what happens to you. Don't you see the dangers you were in tonight? You could have had a wreck because you were driving drunk. Or you could've been arrested for DUI and Minor in Possession. Hell, you could've gotten so drunk that someone could rape you and you wouldn't even know it. You're not invincible like you seem to think you are!" Dana stammered. "And you are all I have." She began to sob again.

Lola stepped closer to her mother. "I'm sorry, Mom." She lowered her head.

Dana reached for her and grabbed her to pull her into a hug. "Please. Please. Stop hurting yourself. It's killing me to watch this."

"Okay, I'll try to be better." Lola sighed and went upstairs to her room.

Dana continued to cry after she left. She put her hands on her face and shook her head. "What am I going to do?" She worried about Lola, but she also worried about herself. She must be going crazy.

Saturday morning started with an early wake-up so she could go with her Science UIL Team to a competition in a city an hour away. The plan called for meeting the students in the parking lot of the school at seven. But someone moved her keys. Dana distinctly remembered putting them down right by her purse on the counter when she came in. She picked up her purse and looked under it. She looked under the counter in case they had fallen off. She began to panic. Where could they be? She turned everything upside down in complete frustration. An odd feeling came over her and a chill went up her spine as she remembered the black mist from the night before. She looked toward the TV and saw a glint of metal on the floor to the side of it. Her keys sat on the floor, arranged so that they looked like a tarantula. Each key pointed down into the carpet with the gold medallion they were attached to resting on top of them. A scorpion rested nearby them. Dana stared at the sight for a few seconds before she could bring herself to step on the scorpion and touch the keys. She grabbed them and shook them to get them out of the odd configuration. Realizing that she was late, she ran out the door and raced to the school.

The normally well-behaved students immediately started fighting as the trip began. Usually, her team members traveled together without any problems as they listened to their music. But this time, her team erupted in a fight over every little thing. Leti wanted to stop at a particular convenience store where she could buy a certain brand of energy drink. Sonya, however, had other plans. She demanded to stop at a different store where her current boyfriend worked. Unfortunately, that store failed to carry Leti's energy drink. The other members of the team took sides and before Dana knew it, war broke out between the two factions. Dana solved the problem by stopping at neither store. She stopped at a different store and the entire team sulked over it. Dana decided that they must all be having PMS, even the boys. But as they got further away from town, they started apologizing to each other and had made up by the time they reached the completion.

The entire day flowed smoothly, that is, until they approached home. Once again, petty bickering broke out and by the time the students exited the van, they were no longer speaking to each other. Dana thought about that for a moment. The fighting among the students had increased daily for the entire week. And yet, when they left town, they loved each other again. She shook her head. And what was it with this headache? It tortured her all week and she still had it this morning. But it disappeared while she traveled with the students, reappearing five miles out of town on the return trip. It must be something she was allergic to around here. Maybe the students had the same allergies and they were feeling bad. Who knew?

Dana picked up her phone as she drove home and called Lola. For a few seconds she worried that Lola would not answer, but finally she did.

"Hi Mom. I'm getting ready to leave."

"Are you going to Amy's party?" Dana wanted to encourage Lola to be around Amy as much as possible.

"No. We have play practice again tonight."

"Again?"

"Yes. The play is next week. We have to get it down."

Dana really wanted to trust her daughter but she just could not do it. "Lola, you're not going to the Red Bridge again are you?"

"No, Mom. I promise."

Not wanting to get into another argument with Lola, she took a deep breath. "Okay. Please be careful. I love you."

"Love you too, Mom."

Dana pulled the car over on the shoulder. She did not want to go home if Lola was not going to be there. She suddenly felt so alone. The events of the past week unnerved her and she questioned her sanity. She needed to talk to somebody, but whom could she trust enough to tell them all the things that had happened. So, she talked to God.

"God, I know you have seen all of these things. Where are you? Please make it stop. And protect Lola from herself and those delinquents she is running with. Please send me some help." She dropped her head. Who was she kidding? God was not listening to her. She took a deep breath as her eyes filled with tears. Did God even exist? Then, she shuddered at the thought of that. It meant that she was really alone.

She did a U turn and headed back to town. She did not know where she wanted to go but she kept driving. Maybe she would see someone she knew at the Burger Place. At least she would not be alone. Looking through the glass walls of the Burger Place, she saw only a few people eating but she decided to go in anyway. She parked her car and walked in, pretending to be interested in the menu above her. Debbie stepped up from behind the counter.

"Can I help you, Mrs. Fleming?" Debbie smiled. She had not seen her ex-teacher there for a while.

"Uhmmm. What's good?"

"Let's see. The newest thing on the menu is the Super Grande Burrito. It's a little spicy but it tastes great. You want to try it?"

Dana was not really hungry but she nodded to Debbie and shrugged slightly. Debbie smiled again. "You want a drink too?"

"Sure, can you get me some coffee?" Dana had a feeling it might be a long night and maybe the coffee would chase away the chill she was feeling.

"Yes, ma'am!"

Dana paid for her meal and turned to find a seat. Luke sat alone at a nearby table and he motioned Dana to come sit with him. Dana did not know Luke very well, but she did not want to sit alone so she smiled and settled into the seat across from him.

"Luke, I haven't seen you for some time. What have you been doing?"

Luke shifted uneasily in his chair. He did not know many women and he was beginning to wonder why he had invited Dana to sit with him. Women made no sense to him and that fact made them a little scary. And, he certainly did not want to discuss the fact that he had just finished burying his beloved dogs. "Oh, just ranchin. How's school?"

Now it was Dana's turn to shift in her chair. She smiled her best fake smile. "Oh, it's been a little wild over there lately, but it's okay."

Her reply surprised Luke and he wanted to know more. "What do you mean 'wild'?"

Dana had not meant to discuss her issues at school with anyone. And yet, she really wanted to talk to someone. She looked at Luke and wondered. Why not? "There's something in the air and the kids are crazy this week. I keep thinking it's the weather, but the weather changed and the kids just kept acting out."

"Like what?"

"Like fighting with each other over everything. They're going off on each other over every little thing. It's like the entire school needs to take a chill pill."

Luke gave a little laugh. He liked Dana's honesty. It was not something he was used to seeing in women. "Maybe they just need a break. When is the next holiday?'

Dana shook her head. "Not soon enough! And that goes for me too!" She looked at Luke across the table and realized that talking to him relaxed her somewhat. He was nothing like her ex-husband. A simple, unassuming air surrounded him and it made it easy to talk to him. Why had she not noticed him before? Maybe the dirty blue jeans and faded T-shirts he wore camouflaged his charm. "So, are the sheep being rebellious too?"

Luke's smile dropped. He took a deep breath and confessed something he had not told anyone else. "What's left of my sheep is being slaughtered daily. I already lost most of my herd."

Dana suddenly realized that she had been so wrapped up in her own problems that she had not thought that others might be having problems worse than her own. Seeing the despondent look on Luke's face made her begin to understand what the loss of an entire herd would do to a rancher. "Oh," she stammered. "I'm sorry to hear that, Luke. Is it coyotes?"

"Yeah...no...I mean, not normal coyotes." He could not believe he had just uttered those words. Now, he would have to explain them. Sure enough, Dana frowned and looked confused.

"What do you mean 'not normal coyotes'?"

Luke studied Dana's face as Debbie brought her meal to her. Would she believe him if he told her what had happened? Surely she would think he was crazy. Maybe he was. Or, maybe it would be good to share it with someone who might not tease him about it like his buddies would. "Damnedest thing. I never saw anything like it before. The coyotes out there have mutated or something."

Now Luke had piqued Dana's curiosity. "What do you mean? Mutated how?"

"They're huge and they run in a pack. They kill just to kill. Very little is eaten." He stopped short of describing the glowing eyes of the coyotes. "They ain't normal."

"You've got to be kidding. Only, I know you're not. One of my students just told me she had seen something like that last Thursday over at Genie Nixon's place. I didn't want to believe her, but if you've seen them too, well...that's a different story."

Luke could hardly believe his ears. Dana had just confirmed that he was not crazy. Someone else had seen these beasts too. Did he dare tell her the entire story? She seemed willing to listen and even believe. "That ain't all. They have glowing eyes and there's an Alpha. Damned thing looks like a prehistoric wolf or something. They attacked me out at my ranch and I just barely escaped."

Dana nodded as she dabbed the sweat gathering on her face because of the spicy meal. "Yeah, April said they had glowing eyes and they were attacking Genie's goats. Wow. I never would have believed it."

"They killed my two guard dogs too. I ain't ever seen anything that could do that."

Silence fell between them as they both digested the true meaning of what they had just discussed. Dana knew that Luke ran with Ignacio.

"Has Ignacio said anything about seeing them? What did he say when you told him what you saw?"

Luke shook his head. "Naw. I never told him about it. I thought I was just seeing things or going crazy. In a way, I'm glad to know somebody else saw it too. But then, that makes them real and that's not good either."

As much as Dana did not want to admit it, Luke's coyotes only confirmed to her that something was very wrong around her little town. But, she was not ready to confess that she had been seeing black shadows. Seeing mutated coyotes was one thing. Seeing demons was another. "I wonder where they came from." She thought for a moment. "Do you suppose they are wolf hybrids?"

"I thought about that possibility too. Still, I never knew wolves to have glowing eyes."

"True. That's really weird." Dana thought for a few seconds. "I've seen some other things that I have never seen around here before."

"Really? What?"

"I came around a curve in the path along the creek when I was going for a run and ran into this gothic-looking collection of huge black vultures sitting on those dead trees in the creek. They all just stared at me and I had to leave."

"The creek, you say? That must have been a bit unsettling."

Dana gave a small laugh as she pushed her plate to the side. "Yeah, but I am sure glad I didn't run into any mutated coyotes! I'd have had a heart attack right then and there."

"I felt like I was going to die right there. The look in the Alpha's eyes showed nothing but hate and I was sure he wanted to kill me. Strange thing is...they just vanished suddenly."

"Wow."

"Yeah, wow. I haven't been out there after dark since then."

"I don't blame you! I'd be afraid to go in the daytime."

Luke confessed. "I ain't gonna lie. It creeps me out, even in the daytime." Somehow, just confessing this to Dana made him feel better about it. She had managed to set him at ease. He had not had a conversation this long with a woman for as long as he could remember. It reminded him of his ex-wife, before she changed. He had to admit to himself that he had missed it. He smiled. "Well, we'll have to watch out for all this weird stuff happening around here. Who would've thought that anything this exciting could happen in this stuffy old town?"

Dana laughed. "Yeah. I thought I was the only one noticing odd things around here. What do you suppose it all means?"

Luke shook his head and shrugged. "Dunno. Just do not know."

They continued to visit as they finished their drinks. By now, the sun had begun to creep down into the west and Dana did not want to get home in the dark. "It looks like the sun is going down. I want to get home before dark," she grinned, "especially now that I have to look out for mutated coyotes."

"Sorry. I didn't mean to scare you. But thanks for the visit. I enjoyed it."

"Me too. Take care of yourself out there, Luke."

"Yeah, you too."

Luke watched as Dana got into her car and drove off. Then he gathered his hat and coat and headed for the door. "Bye, Debbie. See you tomorrow!"

"Bye, Luke. Tomorrow!" Debbie intoned cheerfully. As soon as Luke had left, Debbie turned and faced the kitchen to hide her face. She had listened to every word of Luke's conversation and it scared her. Could it have been the coyotes that had gotten into the Burger Place that night?

She continued her cleanup as she got ready to close for the night. After checking the back door several times to make sure it was locked, she turned out the lights and looked carefully around the parking lot. She stepped quickly to her car and locked the doors after she climbed in. She felt it too. Something eerie saturated the atmosphere.

CHAPTER 13

Amy hurried to prepare the guesthouse for the party. The sun reached the horizon and the girls would be there soon to get the night going. Amy lit candles and checked on the cheese dip in the slow cooker. The sound of tires rolling on the caliche road announced that some of her guests were arriving.

She threw open the door and called out, "It's about time! What took so long?"

Heather laughed. "April and Savannah took forever getting ready. And we stopped at the store to get some snacks."

"Snacks? I have plenty of food already." Then she wondered, "What did you bring?"

"Gummy Bears and Monster drinks. What else?"

"Come on! Alexis and Jacquelyn are on the way. They're bringing the pizza, but we can start eating everything else now."

The girls positioned themselves in the small kitchen area of the cabin, filling their cups with ice and drinks and loading chips and dips onto their plates. Then, they settled onto the couches in the living area. Alexis and Jacquelyn arrived and the girls gathered in the kitchen area again, piling pizza on their plates and laughing.

"Hey, turn on the music," April yelled over the voices.

"Sure. Just a sec." Amy put on the music and the girls raised their voices to be heard above it.

"Louder!" Savannah motioned to Amy.

Amy laughed and turned up the volume. The tiny house vibrated now to the fast beat of the music and the girls got up and started to dance. April started laughing. "Look! Savannah looks like she just sat on an ant hill!" She tried to copy Savannah's style, exaggerating her moves.

Heather yelled over the music, "No, it's more like this!" She threw herself wildly around the room and the others collapsed in laughter.

"Uhm, Amy?" Alexis stared out the window into the dark. Amy did not hear her so she raised her voice, "Uhm, Amy?"

"What?" Amy noticed that Alexis had stopped dancing and looked petrified. She followed Alexis' gaze and her eyes widened. She rubbed her eyes and looked again. A pair of what looked like red eyes stared back at her and she could make out the outline of someone dressed in all black. She ran to the door of the little house and opened it to see more clearly. Whatever it was had disappeared, so she closed the door and shrugged to Alexis.

"There's nothing there. It must've been a reflection from car lights on the highway."

Alexis gave her a relieved smile and turned to look out the window again. Sure enough, the eyes were gone. But she noticed something further away in the pasture. "Uhm, Amy? There's something out in the pasture."

Amy then realized that Alexis was looking at the pasture lights. She danced over to Alexis and put her hands on Alexis' shoulders. "Oh, those are the pasture lights. We see those all the time. Don't worry about them."

Alexis looked back at Amy. "What are they? I have never seen anything like that before."

"We don't know what they are but they never do anything but fly around out there."

Alexis seemed to be happy with the explanation. At least they did not look like they had red eyes. Suddenly, a loud crash came from the cabinet in the kitchen. Amy frowned as she walked over to it and opened it. The large mason jar that her mother used to store her brushes had fallen and broken. As she stared at it, she wondered what had made it fall. Just behind the broken jar, a small piece of the wood at the back of the cabinet began to glow. She stepped back at the sight and put her hand over her mouth. The glowing intensified and then another area about five inches from it also began to glow. The space between them blackened and a face formed around them. Two scorpions fell from the cabinet. She screamed and jumped back.

When Alexis saw what Amy was screaming at, she shot up from the couch and turned to run outside, but what she saw stopped her in her tracks. A purple light flew towards the house and swerved close to the window. Alexis screamed and then fell silent, her eyes wide in fear. The orb reacted by passing through the window, stopping to hover immediately over her head. Alexis shrieked again and threw her arms up over her head. All the girls stopped dancing and turned toward Alexis, dropping their mouths open. They screamed in unison.

Suddenly, many different pasture lights descended on the house and flew erratically around the room, diving at the girls as they ducked and held their arms above their heads. The music transformed to a loud buzz, intensifying as the orbs began to gather and move towards the cabinet. Stooping to keep low, the girls panicked and knocked over the coffee table and some chairs. Pizza and drinks became airborne and landed on the carpet as the girls fled into the bedroom and slammed the door. The girls, now crying, crowded around the bedroom door, holding it closed and screeching every time the buzzing increased in the other room. The pandemonium in the living room continued for a few minutes and then stopped abruptly. The girls looked at each other.

Heather hugged the outer edge of the group. "Are they gone?"

April, who stood the closest to the door, placed her ear on it to listen. THUD! Something heavy hit the door, sending the girls to the floor in a pile. April rubbed her ear. "Oh, hell no!"

They clung onto each other, shaking and crying, for a very long time. Finally, April stood up. "Let's check it out." She slowly turned the handle on the door and began to peek out. Then she poked her head out, scanned the living room and squashed a scorpion with her shoe. "I think they're gone."

The girls moved together through the door, surveying the room as they entered it. Paper plates, pizza and plastic cups lay scattered on the floor. The lamp slumped sideways and leaned on the wall. All the candles had been blown out. It looked like a war had occurred. Silence filled the room. Amy walked over to the living room window and peered out. She saw that the lights were nowhere in sight. "Come on!" she yelled and she bolted out the front door. Her guests followed, scrambling up the hill to her house.

Dedra came down the stairs when she heard the commotion at the front door. The door burst open and the girls all started talking at once, trying to tell her what had just happened. She raised one hand in the air. "Whoa...one at a time."

Amy spoke up first. "Mom! There was something in the cabinet with glowing eyes and then the lights...they attacked us!"

"What?"

"They attacked us, Mom. They came into the house."

Dedra looked at Amy and saw the terror in her eyes. The rest of the girls watched Dedra for her reaction. "Really? They came into the house? They've never done that before. Why would they do that now?"

Amy feared that her mother was not going to believe her. "I don't know. But, can we stay over here?"

"Sure." Dedra frowned. Why would Amy tell her that if it did not happen? The thought of the lights invading the guesthouse concerned her. What if they invaded the main house? She quickly glanced out the door towards the pasture and then closed the front door as the girls climbed the stairs to Amy's room. Then she peeked out the window towards the pasture and saw only a couple of snakes slithering their way toward the pasture. She locked the door. Then she checked it again.

THE HOLE IN THE SKY: PORTAL ONE

CHAPTER 14

After Dana got home from the Burger Place and her conversation with Luke, she waited impatiently for Lola to get home. She called her several times and thankfully, Lola answered each time, sounding a little more perturbed with each call. Finally, Lola arrived home and Dana took a deep breath. Now, she could sleep.

But when she climbed into bed, she could not go to sleep. She felt something strange and almost feared closing her eyes. At least she was not alone tonight. Just the fact that Lola was asleep upstairs helped Dana relax a little. Finally, she closed her eyes.

The sound of barking and growling dogs outside her window pulled her from her sleep. She glanced at the clock. It read three in the morning. Rubbing her eyes, she stepped out of bed and walked silently to the window. Raising the blinds with her finger, she peered out into the darkness. She saw the forms of Buddy and Sam sprinting back and forth across the yard as they barked hysterically at something beyond the fence. She strained her eyes to see what was upsetting them so badly.

Then she saw something move behind a brush thicket just a few feet beyond the fence. She could not see what it was, only that it was dark-colored and big. Dana gasped. What if it was one of those mutated coyotes?

She ran down the hall and flipped on all of the outside lights. Then she ran back to her bedroom and fumbled under the bed for her gun. She ran back to the window to look out again. The dogs continued to react to whatever it was that was out there, but she could not see anything this time. She thought about stepping outside to get a better look, but then shuddered and changed her mind. She opened the door just long enough for the dogs to race into the house with their tails tucked, and then she slammed the door and locked it. At least she had a door between herself and whatever was out there.

Eventually, the dogs settled down beside her and Dana yawned. She really needed her sleep so she checked all of the locks once again and climbed back into her bed. But sleep evaded her. Each time she closed her eyes, she saw fangs moving toward her. She forced her sleepy eyelids open and looked all around her room. Then she pulled her bedspread up and around her neck as close as possible. Finally, her exhaustion caught up with her and she fell asleep.

Dana startled out of her sleep and quickly flipped over onto her back. The light of the sun peaking through the blinds let her know that it must be late in the morning. Taking a deep breath, she looked around her room and smiled. Whatever terror lurked in the night had apparently disappeared.

She checked the clock on her bed stand and realized that she had slept too late to go to Church. Then she frowned. Why did she even go to Church anyway? The events of the past few weeks weighed heavily against her faith and she began to question if God was real. She lay on the bed thinking about all the bad things that had happened to her. Despite her good intentions and attempts to live a good life, fate attacked her at every turn.

All the valiant effort she had given her marriage had failed. She loved and took very good care of her husband, doing everything she knew to please him and keep him happy. Still, he turned his affections from her and cheated with a younger woman. And now Lola followed in his footsteps. Dana knocked herself out to provide Lola with all she needed and all she could get back was hate and fake love. Dana could see that Lola would soon leave her just like her father did, regardless of how good a mother she was. A tear formed and dripped onto her pillow.

How could God be real? If He was real, why didn't He help her? Why even doubt it? She was alone. Nobody cared what she went through. Nobody would help her out of any of it. She took a deep breath. But she knew for sure that evil was real after she had seen the events of the last few days. What if that was all there was...evil? Why should she even try to struggle against it?

She shook her head as if to clear it. No. She could not let herself listen to that. She climbed out of bed and got dressed, determined to prove that she could and would live a good life. If nobody else cared about her, she would care about herself. And that would have to be enough.

After deciding to let Lola sleep in to avoid a confrontation, she busied herself with the mundane chores of laundry, cooking and cleaning for the rest of the day. She would take care of herself and keep herself comfortable, even if nobody else cared about her. This thought strengthened her and soothed her as she went about her chores. Lola came downstairs at a little after one in the afternoon and settled on the couch in the living room. The extra sleep seemed to put her in a better mood and Dana was able to have a pleasant afternoon in her company. Dana successfully managed to avoid thinking about fear...until night fell again. She killed two scorpions on the wall next to her bed and tossed fitfully the entire night.

CHAPTER 15

MONDAY

Monday morning's stress failed to erase the horrible weekend from Dana's mind. She awoke from her fitful sleep seemingly unable to do the simplest tasks. Getting Lola up and moving proved to be even more difficult for some reason. Brain fog made fixing breakfast for Lola a challenge and getting ready for the day difficult. Then, once again, she could not find her keys. Remembering where she had found them before, Dana searched the area around the TV. Sure enough, the keys sat in the very same spot and in the very same configuration that she had found them in on Saturday morning. She shook her head and refused to try to understand that.

She got to school, turned on all of the computers and prepared for the day. The students began to filter into the classroom, moving as slowly as possible. Nobody smiled. It was definitely a Monday. When the tardy bell rang, Dana began her lesson.

Looking out to the sea of exhausted faces, she noticed that Amy looked particularly ragged. She tried to pull herself and her students out of the stupor of the morning. "Good morning!" The students just moaned in response. "Okay, not-so-good morning. I agree, but we have to get started."

Her students looked up at her and grimaced, but she began the class with her usual science current event. This one involved a particular asteroid that would be passing closely to Earth within the week and the students began to show some interest. Then, she went on to her lesson and explained how acids should be named. She assigned the class to do some practice problems while she was there to help them and she began to walk around the room watching the students work.

When she got to Amy's desk, Amy shifted in her seat and looked up at her. "Mrs. Fleming, can I talk to you?"

The look on Amy's face told Dana that something was bothering her. "Sure. Come on up to my desk." Amy walked up to Dana's desk and sat down in the chair at the side of the desk. Dana remembered that Amy had told her about the party she was having at her house. Dana had not heard how it had gone since Lola had not gone to it. "So, how was your party?"

"That's what I wanted to talk to you about. You know how we talked about things we don't understand and how we have to keep an open mind?"

"Yes?"

"You're going to have to keep an open mind while you listen to this."

Dana frowned. What could possibly have Amy saying that? "Okay."

Amy took a deep breath. "I don't know where to start. We were all having a great time and then something happened."

"Like what?"

"See, we have these lights on our ranch that are like the Marfa lights."

"Oh, yes. Your mother told me about those. I want to come see them."

"You might want to rethink that. They're not as harmless as we thought."

Dana watched Amy's face as she struggled to get the story out. "What do you mean?"

"They attacked us that night at the party."

"They attacked you? How?"

"They came into the house and dove down at us. And... there was something very black with glowing eyes that came out of the kitchen cabinet."

By this time, the rest of the students had stopped working and were staring intently up at the desk. Dana looked out into the class at the terrified faces watching her. "Really?"

April spoke up. "We all saw it. They were diving on us. And the music turned to static every time they did it."

Trying to be the science teacher, Dana replied, "Static. That means they have some sort of electrical power to them."

By now, April had stood up. "They had enough power to knock things over and bang on the door we were hiding behind."

Dana shuddered inside. She had never heard of anything like that. "Did anyone get hurt?"

Amy shook her head. "No, but we all ran to the main house as soon as they left. I'm never going there again!"

"Me either!" added Heather.

Dana knew she needed to be the strong one here, but she did not feel very strong after her weekend. She took a breath. "Obviously something really happened. But I've never heard of anything like that. The lights are supposedly like the Marfa Lights, but the Marfa Lights have never attacked anyone that I know of. I wonder what made them do that?"

"Well, we did have the music on really loud," Amy conceded.

"Hmm. Maybe the energy of the music attracted them. There could be all kinds of explanations for that. We just don't have any facts about them." She looked out into the class again and realized that she needed to turn the fear into something else. "You know, the Science Fair is coming up. That would be a great subject to study. You could build in some controls and see if the lights will react to different levels or types of music."

The class just looked at her. Finally, Heather spoke up. "Personally, I'm not going to do anything that attracts those things to me.....ever."

"Yeah. Me either." Amy shook her head.

Putting on a brave front, Dana laughed. "Too bad. You could have a true discovery there." But inwardly, she was glad that she was not going to be dragged into anything like that. "What a wonderful mystery!" she intoned, trying to be as positive as possible for them.

When the class left, she sat down in her chair. *What is going on around here?* The day progressed and the grouchy students fought over everything the entire day. This did not help Dana's constant headache. She rubbed her temples and opened a drawer to find an aspirin. She jumped back in horror. Writhing scorpions filled the drawer and began tumbling out onto the floor. She screamed and looked for something to use as a weapon. When she looked back, the scorpions were gone. *I must be losing my mind!*

After the students left the school for the day, Dana begrudgingly hurried to the meeting that had been called about the coming Homecoming Dance. She stepped into the room and saw that everyone else was already there and she was late. The other teachers in the room looked up at her and then looked back at the agenda that had been given out for the meeting. Nobody smiled. Nobody even acknowledged that she had entered the room. *They must all have the same headache I have,* she thought.

She sat down and put her things on the table. Then, she immediately drifted mentally away from the meeting. She wanted to get on home to be there when Lola showed up. She shook her head. How was she supposed to be a good parent? This job kept dragging her away from Lola at every turn. She resented the fact that she was required to do so many extracurricular things, as if teaching science and having to prepare labs was not enough. Between the UIL practice, the Junior Class sponsorship and putting on the Homecoming Dance, she could not have any quality time with her daughter.

When Lola failed to do her work or acted inappropriately, Dana knew that the others in the room blamed her for it. All of the other teachers, it seemed, had husbands and families to help with some of the burden of raising children, but she was on her own. It did not help that she knew the others were talking about her. Not her really, but about her husband. She knew they thought that she did not know about her ex-husband's recent exploits with the local slut. They looked at her with pity in their eyes, but never offered to help or talk to her about it. It was like they thought she did something to deserve it.

But she could not help it if her husband had cheated on her and left her broke and by herself to raise their daughter. And it was not her fault if her daughter was bent to be just like her father. These people in this room with her did not care about her at all. Nobody did.

A sudden change in the intensity of the voices around her snapped her out of her pity party. The others were now arguing over something. Dana listened to hear what had stirred such a controversy. Apparently, nobody else wanted to have to do the work for the Homecoming Dance either. They bickered over who spent how much time doing what for the dance. As the argument ensued, the overhead lights began to flicker and a sick feeling came over Dana as she looked up at them. Suddenly, the room became very warm.

Sunni Len Cates, a history teacher, pointed her finger toward Dana. "Well, she hasn't volunteered any time yet!"

Dana frowned. "What do you mean? You know I will go when you need me!"

"Everyone else has signed up for a time to decorate, but you haven't! You need to do your part!"

"Fine!" She tugged at her collar in response to the heat. " Just sign me up for whenever you want me to be there!...... That's what you all do anyway!"

She slammed her book on the table, scooted her chair out and headed to the door. She made sure she slammed it after she walked through it. After making it down the hallway, she pushed the double doors and stomped out of the building toward her car. *They can sit in there all afternoon if they want to. I don't give a damn! I'm not hanging around for them to beat up on me!*

She threw her things into the car and climbed into it, pulling the door hard. She had to get away. On automatic now, she drove down the main street and turned toward home, still fuming.

But as she approached the home of the 'watchers', the sight before her made her almost forget her anger. Dwayne and Donny stood on opposite sides of the road, both staring intently toward the West. She followed their gaze and saw that the object of their attention was that peculiar place in the sky. With the majority of the sky obscured with clouds, the hole remained clear again, but this time, radiant beams of light poured out to the ground in stark contrast to the darkness of the cloudy day.

Then, she noticed the expressions on the faces of the boys. With their eyes open wide, they wore huge smiles, like they were looking at a pile of gold or something. Dana frowned. She had never seen the boys with these expressions. As she drew closer to them, they turned toward her and their faces morphed. Suddenly, their eyes narrowed and evil grins replaced the smiles. They locked eyes with her and glared as she passed. *What the hell is wrong with them today?* She knew that they normally smiled and waved as she drove by every afternoon. She had not seen them at school today. Did they spend the entire day out there? She would have to look into that tomorrow. She felt their stare follow her all the way to her turnoff. She shivered as she escaped their gaze.

Looking instinctively in her rearview mirror, she took a deep breath. She began to talk audibly to herself. "Okay, Dana. Stop it! You're going crazy or something. You've got to get it together or they're going to haul you off to some mental hospital."

Purposefully taking slow, deep breaths, she drove on toward her home. What had her so upset anyway? It had to be her problems with Lola that had colored her world and made her stress over everything. That must be the reason she was hallucinating. She scratched her head. But it seemed like everyone else must be hallucinating too. "Well, I can only take care of my own problems."

Lola consistently made poor choices and Dana knew it could really hurt her. Dana did not want Lola to be hurt by men like she had been. "They *all* want only one thing. And then they cheat on you and leave you alone to handle the world by yourself!"

She remembered saying the same words to Lola, but Lola responded with anger against her mother. So far, Dana had not approved of a single boy that Lola had been interested in. Lola hated it when Dana pointed out all of their faults and told her how they were all like her father. It was the flashpoint for almost all of their arguments and Lola always responded by storming out of the house. Sometimes she sneaked out....just like her father.

She turned off the highway when she got to the front drive of her home and got out to open the gate. Her hair blew into her eyes and mouth as she talked to herself and pushed it open. "What am I going to do with her?"

Sure enough, Lola was not home yet. The '92 sedan she drove was nowhere in sight. "I told her to be home by 6... but so what? She doesn't have to do anything I tell her... she's her own woman!" she muttered. There was always just too much to do. Lola did not help matters. Now she would have to try to find her. That meant calling around to all of her friends' houses.

She carried her briefcase past the greeting dogs and the stubborn lock, into the house, grumbling.

She opened the front door and slammed it shut. Dropping her purse and books on the floor, she flung herself onto the couch and closed her eyes. Then, the tears began, slowly at first. Before she knew it, she was sobbing loudly. *I just can't do this anymore!*

She gathered her wits and decided to calm down. All her fears left her powerless against all of the evil coming against her. She began to speak to the air. "I give up! I just can't fight it anymore, God! Lola is going to do what Lola is going to do, just like her father. And now I'm going crazy on top of everything. And I'm so alone. God? Do you hear me? Do you even care? I know you see all of this. And yet, you do nothing. Why have you let me get into this place?"

She remembered what had brought her to this house in the first place. The thought of living peacefully in the country had lured her out here. How could such a lovely dream turn into such a monstrous nightmare? Even when her husband had left her, she tried to make her dream stay alive. She just wanted to be a good mother and teacher. But she realized now that she could be neither in her present state.

The purring engine of her daughter's car announced Lola's arrival. Lola opened the front door and headed straight to the kitchen. "Hi, Mom... what's for supper?"

"Whatever you want to help me cook."

"Uh, I'm supposed to go help decorate the homecoming float."

"Fine...after you help me."

"Mom, I can't. I only have twenty minutes to get back with the posters."

"Oh... the posters... of course!" Dana knew the routine too well. Lola was in a hurry all right, but probably not to get back with the posters to decorate a float. Tanya and Mel were waiting for her somewhere. Dana knew very little about their activities. She knew where they said they were going, but she also knew that they could not be found there. She knew Lola's clothes smelled like smoke, but Lola always explained that the smoker was someone she gave a ride in her car that day.

Lola lied… just like her father.

So, Dana tried again. "I want you to stay home and finish your homework tonight. Mrs. Oliver told me you have an Algebra test tomorrow and you know you have a 72 average."

Lola's sweet smile changed to an astonished frown. "What! No, I turned in some papers today… my average went up… and I know how to do all that stuff on the test."

"Fine… I'll help you with your science project…you know it's due next week."

Lola's eyes rolled up and her voice got louder. "Mom! I have to go! All the sophomores are supposed to help with the float."

"Oh… Right!! The float! Come off it, Lola. I know you better than that! You must think I'm so stupid. Just like your father did! You think I don't know what you do! Just like your father!"

Lola raised her hands up in mock resignation and turned toward the door. "Oh, not AGAIN! I'm not Dad! Why can't you stop saying that! Ahh!" she screamed. The slamming of the door vibrated the old ranch house windows in a thunderous chorus.

Dana's stomping renewed the rattling of the windows with each step as she made her way to the front door. She grabbed the door and flung it open so hard that it crashed into the wall and came bouncing back to hit her.

"Get back in here! I'm not finished with you!" she yelled so hard her voice cracked.

"Yes, you ARE!" was all Dana heard over the gunning engine as Lola spun out in the caliche drive.

Dana grabbed her hair with both of her hands as her angry face crumbled into sobs. The dogs, who had been cowering against the fence, now ran up licking her as she folded to the porch floor.

"Get away!" she screamed, pushing them off. The dogs fled over to the fence and stood staring at her. "Oh, go away!" she sobbed.

But she was not talking to the dogs.

She covered her head with her arms, still shaking with unrelenting sobs. A calm came over her as she became very sleepy and drifted to sleep, unmindful of her location. The sun began to creep down and a chill slowly filled the air. The cold began to pull her out of her sleep. The rage gradually slipped away from her and she began to shiver in the light breeze. She raised her head and looked around, steadily returning to her ugly reality. She let out an audible sigh.

The dogs, who were now resting at the edge of the yard, raised their ears at the sound of her heavy sigh. "Okay. I'm sorry I yelled at you. You're the only ones who care about me. I guess I'd better be nice to you." She patted her knees with her hands and called, "Come on! I promise I'll be nice." The dogs cautiously wandered toward her, wagging their tails. She rubbed their heads and patted their backs. It made her feel a little better.

She stood up and turned toward the house. Closing the door behind herself, she hesitated and then locked it. She did not know why the door needed to be locked. She just felt so vulnerable.

But locking the door did not help her apprehension. Lola was still out there somewhere, probably doing everything she could possibly think of to make her mother angry. She started to pick up her phone and call her, but decided to just leave her alone. She sighed again. "Oh, Lord, please watch over her," she prayed. "I can't do it. You have to."

She sat down on the couch and began to go over all the events of her awful day. The more she thought about it, the more nervous she became. Surely, this stuff could not be really happening. But that thought did not make her feel any better. That would mean that all of the shadows and things she had been seeing and feeling were hallucinations. "So which is worse, demons being real or hallucinations?" She could not even answer that question.

An eerie feeling began to creep up her spine again and she looked apprehensively around the room, crossing her arms and holding her shoulders. She stood up and quickly walked to each window, locking it and pulling on it to make sure it did not open. The darkness in the room began to bother her so she systematically went to each light switch and flipped it on. The entire house was lit up. It did not help. She knew she would not feel better until Lola came home...if Lola came home. She closed her eyes and took a deep breath.

The dogs began to bark happily, announcing Lola's car on the caliche road. Dana sprinted to the front windows to look outside. Distant headlights became brighter as the purring sound of Lola's car got louder. Dana took a deep breath.

She met Lola at the front door, actually excited to see her. "I'm so glad you're home!"

Lola's cold glare told the whole story. "Well, I'm not!" She threw her jacket across the couch and stormed into the kitchen.

Dana's need for Lola's companionship surpassed her anger. "Look, Lola. I'm sorry...again. If you only knew the day I had today. I've had this headache all day and I swear something evil is going on around here. Don't you feel it? All the anger at school?"

"Mom! There is no such thing as evil like you're talking about! So you have a headache? That is not because of evil! I have a headache too! It's you!" She frowned. "Your day couldn't have been as bad as my day. My friends all told me about the stuff that happened in your class and how you reacted to it. And they told me that you stormed out of the meeting. I was so embarrassed! Honestly! You have to stop it, Mom! People are going to start talking about you! You're going to be committed or something!"

Anger began to build in Dana. "What did I do that was so bad? You act like I had a bad day just to embarrass you. Actually, you embarrassed me! You embarrass me all the time! That's part of why my day was so bad!"

Lola threw her glass down, shattering it on the floor. "I so get why my Dad left you! You are crazy! All the stuff about God and evil? None of that is real! Quit trying to make me crazy like you. I hate you!" She shook her head and pursed her lips, glaring at Dana as she stomped out of the kitchen and up the stairs.

"You get back down here and clean up this mess!" Dana stood in the middle of the shattered glass and dripping milk, shaking. She closed her eyes and the tears began to flow. "I just want to die." And the sobs came freely. After a few minutes, she took a breath and sniffed, wiping her eyes on her sleeve. Her face assumed a blank stare and she dutifully began to clean up the mess. When was this hell going to end?

The hollow feeling in her stomach ached. She walked to her bedroom in a trance-like state and put herself on automatic as she brushed her teeth and took a shower. Sleep would be next to impossible tonight. She heard Lola's footsteps upstairs as she walked around getting ready for bed too. Every few minutes, a door would slam and the house would shudder in response.

How could Lola be so hateful? Dana wavered between her need for Lola's company and her despair over her ugliness. She felt like she should go up there and just straighten her out. But exactly what would she do or say? Dana knew anything she tried would only escalate the argument, so she decided to just let it go until they both cooled down. Still, the ugly feeling in the pit of her stomach swirled violently in her fear and aching sadness. Was there any hope?

A chill began to build in the house. Dana put on her robe and started to pace. Anxiety drove her to go to each window and door to check the locks. Sure enough, two of the locks she had previously locked had become unlocked. She frowned. *Maybe I do need to be committed. I swear I locked all the windows.*

The upstairs became quiet so Dana stood at the base of the stairs, wondering if she should go check on her daughter. A new sound emanated from Lola's room. Dana had never heard this sound before. She started to climb the stairs slowly. The closer she came to the second floor, the louder the snarling growl became. As she reached the top of the stairs, a true fear gripped her and she stopped breathing to be able to hear it better. The growl coming from Lola's room suddenly turned into a loud gasping snore. Dana let out her breath and laughed at herself. Still, she peeked into the room. Lola had somehow figured out how to sleep despite all the anger. She quietly walked back down the stairs and to her room. She had to try to sleep.

In her dream, Dana found herself much younger and sitting in Church. She knew the church. It was the first church she attended when she moved to her new town. She had pressed her husband to move there in an attempt raise her family in a safer place. The same purpose had driven her to move out to the ranch where she presently lived.

The preacher spoke loudly as he looked out the window. "I was called here on a mission. I am supposed to guard the gateway." He pointed out the window. Dana thought *gateway to what? Guard it from what?*

The loud sound of dogs yelping pierced the night and pulled her from her dream. She leapt out of her bed and raced over to the window, pulling the curtains apart so she could see outside. The hairs on her body stood straight up at the sight before her. Glowing eyes stared back at her from just beyond the fence. Shadows danced around in the yard and when they turned toward the house, their glowing eyes gleamed in a blood red color.

She gasped and dropped the curtains closed. Without thinking, she searched under the bed and grabbed the twenty-two. Then, she hesitated and also reached for the brass cross hanging on the wall. The thunderous growling escalated outside. She froze. Then she jutted out her chin and walked toward the front door. She started to unlock it, but she discovered in her horror that it was not locked. "What the Hell?!" She knew she had locked it...several times. She froze again at the thought of the doors being unlocked again.

A yelp forced her to jump and open the door, frantically swinging the gun back and forth as she searched for any sign of the glowing eyes. She saw nothing so she began to whisper call to the dogs. "Buddy! Sam!" The lack of response forced her to swallow hard. She called louder this time. "Buddy! Sam!"

The sound of running paws around the house caused her to freeze. Was it the dogs, or something else, rushing for her? In an instant, she saw Buddy's golden fur rounding the corner and she took a breath. Sam arrived at the same time. She opened the door wider. "Come on! Get in here! Hurry up!"

The dogs pushed past her and she slammed the door and locked it in one motion. She stared out the window on the door. She shuddered. At least ten sets of glowing eyes stared back at her. The dogs cowered against her legs, seemingly grateful to be behind the door. She moved toward the base of the stairs.

"Lola! Wake up!"

Lola did not answer. Dana ran up the stairs, followed by the dogs, and ran into Lola's room. She turned on the light and Lola moaned. "Lola! Wake up!"

"Oh my God! Mom! What the hell do you think you're doing? What time is it?"

"Uh, I think it's around three. Get up! There are monsters with glowing eyes outside the yard!"

"Ugh! Mom!" She sat up, rubbing her eyes and shaking her head. "What? You're insane!"

"No! They're out there! Come look for yourself!" Dana ran to Lola's window and opened the shades.

Lola frowned and crawled out of bed. She pushed her mother aside and looked out the window. Then, she turned to Dana with her hands on her hips. "What! There is nothing out there! You are seeing things! I told you that you are hallucinating!"

Dana pointed to the dogs. "Do you see the dogs? They saw them too! They were yelping. I had to go save them from the monsters."

Lola dropped her mouth open to say something, then closed it. She took Dana's face in her hands. "You are certifiable! There is nothing out there. Now, leave me alone." She shook her head as she climbed back into bed. "Turn off the light!"

Dana stood there for a second and then turned off the light and walked back down the stairs. The dogs followed her and hopped up onto the couch as she sat down. She looked at them. "You saw them, right? I know you saw them. You were afraid of them, right? I know you were afraid of them." The dogs just licked her hands and cuddled up to her. She laid her head on Buddy's soft head and closed her eyes. *If I'm certifiable, so are these dogs.* A tear formed and fell quietly down onto Buddy's fur.

CHAPTER 16

TUESDAY

Tim loved his job as Sheriff. Most of the time, he worked during the day and let the deputies handle the night shift. But, when his deputy, James Austin, called him at around one in the morning, he knew he would be out all night handling this.

As he left his house, he activated the blue-tooth and called Lloyd Miller, who was the Chief EMT. Lloyd answered sleepily.

"Yeah? What's going on?"

Tim cleared his throat. "Lloyd, send everyone you have to the Four Corners. Multiple stabbings."

"What?!!"

"Yeah, believe it or not, we have had our first gang fight!"

"Gang fight? We don't have any gangs here!"

"We do now! See you there."

Lloyd, along with EMTs Mirza Escamilla and Andy Malinovsky, raced to the scene to find two of the gang members already deceased and six others badly injured. Tim walked up to them as they worked feverishly to slow a bleeding artery.

"What can I do to help?"

Lloyd pointed with his chin over to another victim. "See if you can stop the bleeding from that abdomen over there."

Tim grabbed a handful of gauze and raced over to the young man Lloyd had indicated. He stuffed the gauze into the wound and the young man yelled.

"I know. I know. It hurts, but we have to stop the bleeding." Trying to calm him, Tim asked him, "What's your name, kid?"

"Cas. Cas Garza."

Claudia Ludwig and her friend, Barbara, came up and Lloyd shouted orders to them to help the victims with less deadly wounds. Deputy Hill arrived and began organizing the loading of victims into the two ambulances. Within a few minutes, Lloyd and Mirza were each driving an ambulance to the nearest hospital, thirty miles away. With their clothes stained in bloody patches, Tim and Shane stood watching the taillights of the ambulances as they raced away. Tim's radio suddenly went off.

Penny's voice boomed loudly. "Sheriff! Get over to the Smith's house on Swinney Street. Report of shots fired!"

Tim quickly turned to Shane. "Stay here and take witness reports. I'll call Oscar to help at the Smith house." He knew Border Patrol Agent Oscar Sierra was on duty nearby that night.

He called Oscar. "Oscar, meet me at the Smith's house on Swinney. Shots fired."

Oscar pulled up in his Border Patrol car shortly after Tim got to the house. His Border Patrol dog, Bandit, paced nervously in the back seat of the vehicle as Oscar jumped out to meet Tim on the lawn.

Oscar looked around. "Who called it in?"

"The neighbor, Monica Eicher. "Let's go to the door."

They carefully approached the door and stood to its sides. They listened after they knocked, but no sounds came from within. Tim knocked quietly.

"Mr. Smith? Mrs. Smith?"

Immediately, sounds of shuffling feet and an unlocking door caused Tim to draw his weapon. The door slowly opened to reveal the Smith's young daughter, Pat, who was quietly crying and looking back inside the house in fear. She looked up at Tim.

"Help!", she whispered. "My mother has gone crazy. She shot Daddy. I'm so scared!"

"Where is she?"

"In their bedroom.... over there." She pointed to the left side of the house.

Tim pulled her out of the house by the arm and signaled to Oscar to get her away from the house. He walked slowly into the house, listening for any sounds coming from the bedroom. He heard nothing. The door to the bedroom was open, and he could see the back of Mrs. Smith as she stood there completely still. In front of her was Rickie, her husband, sprawled out on the bed with a gaping hole in his chest and obviously very dead. He located the shotgun on the floor to Mrs. Smith's side.

He ran into the room and kicked the rifle over to the side of the room. Mrs. Smith did not react at all, almost like she had not heard him. He scanned the area for any more weapons but found none.

"Mrs. Smith?"

She did not move a muscle. He still did not trust the situation.

"Mrs. Smith, turn around."

She just stood there staring at Rickie's body.

"Mrs. Smith. Do you hear me?"

She made no movements but he could see that she was trembling. He decided that he had to other choice but to grab her by her shoulders and turn her around to face him. She just stared blankly forward.

"Mrs. Smith!!!!", he yelled. No response.

He yelled toward the front door, "Oscar! Get in here."

Oscar came bounding in with his gun drawn. "What happened?"

"I don't know. She is completely catatonic and Rickie is dead. Where's their son, Aneko?"

As Tim slipped cuffs onto Mrs. Smith's wrists and secured her in the car, Oscar carefully searched the other rooms and found Aneko hiding in his closet. He brought him out to join his sister. They sat the kids down on the sidewalk and began to question them.

Tim looked Pat in the eyes and took her hand. "Tell me what happened."

She shuddered. "They put us to bed and I was sleeping. Then I heard the gun and ran in to see what happened. Daddy's d...d...Dead!" She started sobbing and dove for his shoulder.

After a few seconds, he pulled her away gently. "Had they been fighting?"

"No. They never fight. Everything was good."

Tim pulled Oscar over. "Something isn't right. Janice is the sweetest person I know and she's never been violent. The kids say they weren't fighting. What the hell made her shoot Rickie?"

Before they could answer the question, the radio in the car squawked. Penny's voice called out.

"Be advised that we have now had two reports of peeping Toms with glowing eyes. Yes, that is what I said. Glowing eyes. Both were in the neighborhood of Swinney and Post."

They looked at each other. Oscar frowned. "What the hell?"

Dropping the kids off at the Sheriff's office, they sent Deputy Tex Hill to secure the crime scene at the Smith's house, called the Judge to pronounce Mr. Smith dead and sped towards the location of the glowing eyes incidents. They pulled up to Nita Frasier's house where they could see Nita and the entire family peeking cautiously out the window. The family jumped and ran to the door to welcome Oscar and Tim.

Nita could not wait to tell them what had happened.

"You should've seen it! Really big, bright orange, glowing eyes staring through that window over there. We screamed and they kept staring. Finally, I grabbed the broom and hit the window with it. Then, the eyes disappeared. And our dogs were going crazy and yelping in fear!"

Tim tugged on his hat. "Mrs. Frasier, could it have been a person?"

Mrs. Frasier shook her head.

"Mrs. Frasier, has anyone here been drinking or doing drugs?"

The entire family screamed, "NO!"

Tim looked at Oscar and pulled him away to talk to him. "Any ideas about what this is?"

Oscar shrugged. "That's a big nope."

"Well, let's check out the property and see what we can find."

He looked over at the family. "We're going to check out the property now. Stay inside."

They drew their weapons and started cautiously around the home. The family dogs were barking loudly as they circled the house and found nothing. Oscar grabbed his flashlight and began looking for tracks around the window. Sure enough, the light illuminated several huge paw prints and a snake close to the window. Several large scorpions rested on the window sill. The prints looked like prints from a large dog or a coyote, though they were too large to be from a coyote. Tim ran the snake off and pulled his camera from his pocket and took pictures of the prints as Oscar shined the light on them. They went back to the front door and knocked. Nita answered the door.

"Ma'am, we didn't find anyone lurking around here, but we did find some interesting large dog prints by that window. And several scorpions were trying to get into the window. You might want to call an exterminator tomorrow. We took photos of the prints and we will take them back to the office to study them more. I suggest that you and your family stay indoors and close the blinds to all the windows in case they come back. Call us if they do."

Nita nervously rubbed her arms. "Okay. Thank you, Sheriff. We'll call if we see anything. Let me know what you figure out about the tracks."

"Yes, Ma'am. We will."

When Tim and Oscar went to the next sighting location, the story was the same; scared people, no intruders found, big dog prints and more scorpions and snakes.

Tim looked at Oscar. "Why are there so many scorpions and snakes tonight?"

Just as they got back into the car, Penny's voice sounded over the radio.

"Sheriff, we have a report of a sudden death at Swinney and Lineman... Marie Casalaspro's house."

"We are almost there right now."

Oscar looked at Tim. "This is too odd. It's in a line with our last two calls."

"Yeah.... too odd."

When they drove into the driveway at Marie's house, Marie's husband, Gordon, ran out the door. He reached the car door before Tim could open it.

"She's dead! It scared her to death!"

Tim lifted Gordon's hands off the car door so he could open it. He frowned and looked at Gordon.

"Who's dead?"

The old man practically jumped over to his front door with Tim and Oscar following him. He ran into the house and over to the dining room window, where Marie lay on the floor.

He sobbed, "She's dead!"

Oscar bent down to check Marie out. He stood up, looked at Tim and said, "She's dead, Tim."

He turned to Gordon. "What happened?"

"I was in the bedroom and I heard Marie scream real loud. I ran out to see what was going on and she was standing by that big window, screaming as loud as she could. I looked at the window and saw two huge, glowing eyes looking in the window."

Tim and Oscar looked at each other.

"And then she just fell over dead. I think it scared her to death."

Tim went back out to the car radio. "Penny, get an ambulance over here right now!"

"Yes, sir! But the only ambulances we have are only now returning from the last run."

"Well, when they get back, send them over to the Casalaspro's house. No hurry. Marie has passed away."

"Yes, sir."

He went back into Gordon's house to console him and to let him know that the ambulance would be there before long. He looked at Oscar.

"Well, come on. I have a feeling there'll be more for us to do.... and soon."

Sure enough, the minute they had buckled themselves into the car, the radio squawked and Penny's voice came through again.

"Sheriff, Leigh Castillo just called to confirm what people are telling her." She ran the local newspaper.

"Like what?"

"Like Stacey Ashabranner called to report a pack of big dogs attacking her dogs. Then JoLee McKaskle and Benita Villarreal both called to report a peeping tom with glowing eyes. Theresa Ploesser called to let me know that she heard big cat screams, as in multiple, out at her ranch."

"Why didn't they call us?"

"They did but the number was busy according to Leigh."

"Well, that doesn't surprise me. We *have* been busy! Call her back and tell her we have it all under control. The last thing we need is for people to start panicking."

"Yes, sir."

Oscar looked at Tim. "What if I'm starting to panic?"

Penny's voice called out over the radio in complete panic. "Sheriff!! Major accident on Highway 80! An 18 Wheeler has jack-knifed and there are multiple other vehicles involved!"

Debbie Cortes opened her eyes and waved her arm towards the blaring alarm clock. She found the top of it and silenced it. Then, she rolled to her back and rubbed her eyes. Sitting up slowly, she clicked the lamp on and looked around on the top of her bed. *Now where are those cats?*

Her cats were her children and they usually slept on her bed with her. But, this morning, they were nowhere to be seen. Debbie stood up and walked to the other side of the bed to see if they were over there for some reason. She shook her sleepy head. "Nope."

She frowned and headed to the bathroom. When she came out, she walked out the bedroom door and looked both ways down the hallway. No cats. "Hmmm." Surely, they would be waiting for her in the kitchen for breakfast.

As she entered the kitchen, she realized that the cats were not there either. She called out to them. "Where are you, babies?" After a few seconds, she realized that they were not coming to her call. *That's strange.* They usually made complete pests out of themselves until Debbie opened several cans of cat food for them. So, she picked up a can and began to open it. *That will get them running in here.*

But no cats came running for their breakfast. Debbie knew something had to be wrong now. She put the can down and began to search the house. She went from room to room calling for them. *Where did those cats go?* Finally, she swung open the laundry room door.

All eight of her cats sat entranced at something beyond the door. They did not even turn to look at her when she walked into the room. "Now, what in the world are you doing, babies?"

She stepped forward and, in one coordinated movement, the cats turned and hissed vehemently at her. She stepped back out of the room and just stared at them. They stared back. A sinking feeling came over her and she began to back up out into the hallway. The cats rushed towards her and she slammed the door. Now, they scratched loudly on the door and yowled.

Debbie stood there in the hallway with her mouth hanging open. "Oh my God! What's wrong with them?"

The yowling and scratching stopped suddenly and Debbie stared uneasily at the door. She had to know what was going on. She slowly opened the door and the cats all looked at her and began to meow for their breakfast, rubbing lovingly on her legs.

She looked down at them in wonder. "Okay, that was a funny joke, babies. Don't do that to me. You scared me, you naughty babies."

She waded through the cats as they escorted her to the kitchen in their normal breakfast behavior. She fed them and leaned against the counter, watching them as she frowned. "That was too weird."

She walked back down to the laundry room and went up to the outer door. She pushed aside the curtain to see if she could see anything out there. The sun had begun to rise on the horizon. Everything appeared to be normal out in the yard. *What was out there?*

The rising sun reminded her that she had to hurry now to get to work. She scrambled as she got herself ready and went out the door, locking it behind her. As she drove, she replayed the entire event over in her head trying to figure out her cats' strange behavior. She remembered that she had brought them the meat that had been spilled by the intruder at the Burger Place the night before. Maybe something had contaminated it. No matter how hard she thought about it, she could not understand it. She shook her head. "Weird cats!

Dana jerked awake and looked frantically around her. She realized that she had fallen asleep on the couch, surrounded by Buddy and Sam. Rubbing her eyes, she stretched, causing the slumbering dogs to wake so she went to the door and unlocked it to let them out. She stumbled to the kitchen to make the coffee and called up the stairs to wake Lola. Finishing her coffee and toast, she got herself ready and picked up her briefcase. Once again, she found the keys in their odd placement in the same place she had found them before. She shook her head. *No. I'm not going to be crazy today.*

As she started to pull out onto the highway, she suddenly stopped. A line of cars stretched all the way to Highway 80. She had never seen anything like this as she lived a good three miles from town. She had never seen anything like this in her town ever. The line of cars slowly moved towards Highway 80 and she could see major blockages on it. Sirens and flashing lights encompassed the entire scene. She frowned.

An 18-wheeler lay on its side blocking the entire highway and two SUVs had been seemingly tossed across the median onto the only other path into town. The SUVs had been flattened. Bodies lay covered nearby and Dana noticed several ambulances, including some from the neighboring county. A fire truck sprayed a huge column of water onto the vehicles as the Sheriff and Deputies ran from vehicle to vehicle. Something had caused huge cracks in the highway that continued into the brush. The line of cars came to a complete stop and showed no hope of moving any time soon. She was definitely going to be late.

She got out of her car and walked up onto the scene, finding a group of her ex-students huddled there. They told her that the Sheriff had instructed them to stay there because they were witnesses. She folded her arms as she watched the activity at the scene. Two women walked up to the Sheriff.

"Hello, Sheriff. I'm Mesha Bizzell and this is my friend, Mistie Dawn. We are nurses in San Antonio and we were on our way to work. Is there anything we can do to help?"

Tim bowed his head and shook it. "Ladies, thank you for your kind offer, but all the family members in both cars and the driver of the truck are deceased. As far as I know, there are no other injuries."

"Oh... How horrible.... I'm so sorry. Do we know who the victims are?"

"One family was the Escamilla family. Ez, Ricardo and Ivan. The other family was the Sepulveda family. Erma and her kids, Jesus and Carmen. They were all local people. It's a terrible tragedy. Please excuse me. I need to talk to these EMTs." He turned away from them and headed to the waiting ambulances.

Three ambulances from the neighboring county waited just in case they were needed. Tim walked up to the group of waiting EMTs. He knew David Cheng and Hope and Tyler Vaselovic from previous incidents when they had helped.

"Thanks for coming. I'm afraid there are no survivors to be transported, but we may need to you to transport the bodies."

Hope sighed. "It's just awful. How did this happen?"

Tim shook his head. "The driver of the semi lived for just a few minutes and told us what happened. He said that a pack of coyotes ran out in front of him and he lost control. He said they were huge. Maybe he was hallucinating. Who knows? I'm about to question the witnesses." He shook their hands just before turning to the small group waiting to tell him what they had seen.

Dana, Edward Lewis, Victoria Resendez, Sherry King and Fredo Hernandez stood talking amongst themselves as Tim approached them. They turned to look at him as he approached.

"Hi, Dana. Were you a witness too?"

"Uh...no. I was just talking to them."

Sherry stepped forward. "It was awful! I haven't ever seen anything like it. I was just coming out of Pico's when it happened."

Tim motioned for Oscar to come join him and then pulled out his notepad. "Okay, I need each of you to tell me what you saw."

Sherry continued, "I didn't see what caused it. Maybe it was those huge cracks in the road. All I knew was that there was a terrible screeching of tires and that is when I looked over there. The semi jack-knifed and the whole thing kept skidding towards us fast. Honestly, I was afraid it was going to make it all the way to where I was. But, when it jack-knifed, it hit the two SUVs coming from the other way and sent them flying to where they landed. I ran to try to help. The semi driver, Armand Daniels according to the sticker on the dash, was still conscious. He was muttering something about coyotes and glowing eyes. Then, he died."

Tim and Oscar exchanged glances when the glowing eyes were mentioned. Tim turned to Victoria, who was shivering and rubbing her arms.

"What did you see?"

"I was just walking towards town and I saw pretty much what Sherry said she saw. It all happened so fast! It happened just after the truck passed by me. I thought I was in a movie or something. Crazy."

Tim looked at Edward and Edward frowned. "You're gonna think I'm crazy, but I saw a pack of coyotes run right in front of the truck right before it jack-knifed. They ran across the road away from town. I never knew coyotes ran in packs like that."

Tim looked right at him. "They don't. But, after last night, I might believe anything."

Fredo chimed in. "I saw them too. Dangdest thing I've ever seen. Everything else was like Sherry said."

Tim shook his head and finished jotting his notes down, then he looked up at the group. "Okay. Thanks everybody. I will contact you if I have any more questions."

Dana listened intently to everything everyone was saying. She shuddered. Were those the coyotes that had been terrifying her last night? The accident had occurred only three miles from her house. Were they the same ones Luke had seen? But she did not have time to lose. She was already late, so she got back into her car when she saw that a path had been made for the traffic to pass the wreckage. She started her car and headed toward the school.

She approached the area where the Watchers usually stand along the road. Sure enough, they were there, and not just one at a time like they usually did. The entire family stood there watching, but they were not staring at the wreck. They were staring intently at the hole in the sky..... and they were smiling. Dana tried not to stare as she drove by. *It looks like they are going to be late to school today too.*

CHAPTER 17

As she raced to the school, Dana noticed many of her fellow teachers and the students were still trying to get there too. They would probably have to start classes at second or third period. Pulling into her parking place at the back of the school, she unlocked the back door to her lab and tossed her briefcase and lunch in a heap on her desk. She trotted to the end of her classroom and opened the door, fully expecting to find her class waiting outside for her to let them in. But her students were not there.

Dana frowned as she followed the sounds emanating from the foyer of the building around the corner. The crash of glass shattering onto the floor, followed by the screams of students hastened her steps. The scene she found as she turned the corner was one of complete chaos. Students cowered against the walls covered in glass shards as they sobbed and shivered. Two of her fellow teachers, Carolyn Stoddart and Christine Rideout, stood frozen in front of the now shattered plate-glass windows at the front of the building. She ran up to them.

"What happened?"

Carolyn seemed to snap out of a trance. "I don't know! We were all standing here waiting for everyone else to get here when something hit the glass."

Dana pushed past her to look outside the window. A huge crow lay dead on the ground. "Uhmm. There's a big dead crow out here, but I doubt that it could break this window." She kept searching but found nothing else to explain the break.

One of the students sitting against the wall, Monica Eicher, called out to her.

"Mrs. Fleming, the bird slammed really hard into the glass. I saw it sitting right over on the other building looking at us. Then, it flew up really high and dived straight for us."

Carolyn and Christine looked at Dana and shrugged. Dana decided that it would be best to get the students away from all the broken glass.

"Okay, let's all get to our classrooms. I am declaring it to be Second Period. Everyone go to their classes now. I'll get someone to clean this up."

She pulled out her cell phone to call the office, which was across the street in the other building. The call went through, but static crackled the whole time it was ringing and then the call was dropped. She looked at the phone and saw that she had plenty of bars so the service should have been perfect. She ended the call and tried again. The static buzzed even louder this time.

As she stood there trying to figure out the problem, she noticed that Selma, the office secretary, hurried on her way across the street from the other building. Dana waited until she got into the door, staring at the broken window with her mouth agape.

"Selma, I was just trying to call the office. Is everything alright over there?"

"Mrs. Fleming, the phones are not working. There is too much static so they sent me over here to check on things. But I see that there is a problem.... a BIG problem!"

"Absolutely! A bird crashed into the window. I'm just happy nobody got cut with all the flying glass. The students were right here when it happened. I was trying to call for help but my phone had the static too. Can you please let them know we need someone to get the glass up as quickly as possible, hopefully before class change so nobody gets hurt?"

"Yes, Ma'am. I'll tell them right now." She scooted quickly across the street as Dana returned to her class.

Many of the students were absent. Dana figured that it was due to the accident at the highway. She decided to pull out a video for those who were there to watch instead of leaving half the class behind on the explanation of titration. She put on the video and stepped out the door. As she did, she heard the sounds of sweeping in the foyer and rounded the corner to see Reuben carefully rounding up the glass.

"Hi, Mrs. Fleming. I'll have this all cleaned up in a few seconds. We're going to have to put up some plywood to block the window. The others went to go get some."

"Thank you, Reuben, that sounds like a great plan."

She stepped back toward her classroom but, before she could get in the door, she heard the sounds of students yelling and desks moving mixed with the video. She could not believe her eyes. Mary Duran and Connie Castro were locked in combat, knocking over desks, as the other students yelled at them. She ran into the room and quickly grabbed Mary in a lifeguard lock and began pulling her away as she shouted orders for

Mitzi to grab Connie and keep her away. Once they were separated, the girls continued to scream obscenities at each other. Dedra Boutwell, whose classroom shared a door with Dana's classroom, came running in to see what all the commotion was about. Dana called for her to take Mary off her hands. Dedra's students peeked carefully through the door at Dana's students. Dana stood between the two girls and yelled.

"Everybody Shut Up!!!!!!!"

The entire class, including Mary and Connie, came to complete silence. They had never heard Mrs. Fleming say anything like that. Mrs. Boutwell now stared in shock at Dana. Dana reached over and turned off the blaring video.

"You too!!!!!! Now everyone who is not holding a fighter sit down and stay down!"

The students tiptoed to the desks and picked them up and sat down, keeping their eyes peeled on Mrs. Fleming. She motioned to Mary and Connie, who were now more afraid of Mrs. Fleming than angry at each other.

"Come on, girls. Let's go to the office."

She walked between the girls all the way across the street and to the office, where she seated Mary on one side of the room and Connie on the other. Principal Robert Hibbitts stepped out of his inner office in response to the commotion.

Dana filled him in. "Mr. Hibbitts, these two girls broke into a fight in my classroom. I have no idea what it was about. I don't care what it was about. I only know that they were tossing desks in my classroom right next to the glass cabinets. Now, I'm returning to my class. Hopefully, nobody else will try to kill each other."

Mr. Hibbitts motioned for the girls to enter his office. "What a day it's been! This is the third fight we have dealt with this morning, and we've only been here for two hours. Everybody's in a bad mood, including me!"

"Me too, Mr. Hibbitts. Me too!" Dana turned and stepped out the door. As she walked back across the street, she realized that she had indeed handled the situation badly. She would have never thought to say that to the class. She shook her head. *Between the lack of sleep and this eternal headache, I'm going to get fired!*

She had barely returned to her classroom when the class change bell rang. The students hurried out, looking back cautiously at her and frowning. The next group of students entered the room and they all looked like they had a headache too. What was going on? After deciding that she did not want to get her classes out of sync with each other, she put on the same video and sat at her teacher's desk, brooding. This day could not end soon enough.

Just as she had thought that thought, the fire alarm began to blare and the strobe lights flashed. She knew that this was not a fire drill. The fire drills consisted of the bell ringing three times. To make things more confusing, a recording came over the intercom.

"Please exit the building. A fire has been detected. Do not use the elevator. Use the stairs instead."

The students looked around in confusion. Instead of leaving the room, they whispered to each other. Dana began to freak out again.

"What? What's the problem?", she yelled. "LEAVE. LEAVE NOW!"

Savannah reacted. "But Mrs. Fleming. We don't HAVE an elevator, do we?"

The students began to chatter back and forth.

"I never knew we had an elevator."

"The school only has one floor."

"Where is it?"

Dana had reached her end. "WHAT DIFFERENCE DOES IT MAKE? WE'LL FIND IT LATER!!!! NOW GET OUT!!!!"

Finally, the students quickly exited the building. Groups of students stood in lines all around the building, nervously chattering to themselves. Carolyn and Christine came over to Dana.

Christine whispered to her. "So, where's the fire? Was it in your room?"

"No."

"We all assumed that it would be in the science lab."

"No. I don't know where it was. And what was it with that recording?"

"Yeah...we don't have an elevator do we?"

"No! It's a single-story building for pity sake!"

Dana asked all the other teachers if they knew where the fire was. Nobody had seen a fire. So, she called them together.

"Look. This is ridiculous. I don't see or smell smoke anywhere, do you?"

They all shook their heads.

"I don't think there's a fire. Just a faulty alarm system or something. I'm going in to check it out."

She quickly entered the building and sprinted around, checking each room. She found no evidence of a fire anywhere. She stopped short when she rounded a corner and saw a black shape slip under a door. *No, no, no.... I am not doing crazy today.* She slowly approached the door and quickly opened it. Whatever she had seen had disappeared. *Calm down, Dana. They are going to fire you and lock you away.* About that time, the Fire Department arrived and forced her to leave the building.

"There isn't any fire!" she yelled at them as she exited.

After a few more minutes, the firefighters came out and gave the all-clear. The students meandered back into the building, mumbling and wishing there had been a fire so they could go home. Dana gathered her students and began the video again. But, within fifteen minutes, the video slowed to a stop and all the lights and electricity died. The students let out an audible moan. Without the air conditioner, the classrooms would soon become very stuffy.

Dana stood up in front of the class. "Hold on, hold on. Give it a second. It might come back on."

They all waited, mumbling amongst themselves until Selma suddenly appeared at her door.

"Mrs. Fleming, they don't know why the electricity has gone out. It's only at the school, so they wanted me to come and let you know that we're letting school out early because of it. Let the students know that we'll be closing at noon today, about fifteen more minutes."

"Thanks, Selma."

Dana turned to the students to tell them the good news. They all applauded and began to gather their things. She heard voices in the hallway outside of her door.

"The Ascendance will begin presently. The cogency intensifies. The aperture awaits."

Dana frowned. Who would be using words like that and what were they talking about? She opened the door expecting to find adults.

What she found was The Watchers, in full excitement mode.

Debbie Cortez pulled up in her driveway and quickly ran to the front door. She had forgotten to bring the pictures of her niece's Quinceanera to work to show to Casey. After struggling with the house keys, she pushed the door open and stepped inside. Before she got past the living room, the sounds of a cat growling intensified to the very loud sound of many cats growling. The hair on her arms stood up and she froze where she was standing.

Her cats approached her from the hallway, seemingly stalking her, as they growled in a thunderous unison with hissing interspersed.

"He... hello, my babies......It's only me..... your mommy. Calm down."

Instead of her voice calming them, the growls and hissing became even louder as the cats glared at her with their ears pinned back. She glanced back at the door. Knowing that they could outrun her and would chase her like prey if she ran, she took one step backwards towards the door as she kept her eyes on them. Then, she took another step as quietly as possible. With the third step, the cats moved forward. And with the fourth step, they attacked.

One cat pounced onto her shoulder and began to bite her ear as it dug its claws into the skin of her shoulder and upper chest. Another cat attached itself to her calf and bit hard. Other cats landed on her arms and one even on her head. She knew she had to get away or they would kill her. Spinning around hard, she lost a few of them but not before they managed to leave deep scratches on her arms. She got to the door and pulled it open.

Immediately, the cats dropped off of her and scrambled out the door together, leaving her standing there in shock. The cats ran across the yard and then disappeared through the bushes of the house across the street. Debbie quickly closed the door in case they decided to come back and finish the job. Bleeding from all of her wounds, she stumbled to the bathroom and began to clean them. She applied antibiotic cream to each one and bandaged the ones that kept bleeding. Then, she looked in the mirror at her frazzled appearance.

"What the hell?"

Peeking out the window on the front door, she cautiously looked all around to see if the cats were still there. She saw none, so she slowly opened the door and ran to her car. As she closed the door, she noticed several other cats sprinting in the same direction that her cats had gone. The cats were oblivious of her or anything else as they hurried to some unknown destination. Suddenly, two dogs also appeared, making their way in the same direction. *Oh, My God! What's wrong with all the animals?* She threw her car into gear and decided to go back to work, mainly because she did not want to be alone.

Tim slapped his radio on his leg several times and then pushed the button again. "Oscar....

can you hear me?" The static and scratching only continued. He pulled his cell phone out of his pocket to see if it had suddenly started working. Static. It was just what he needed. As if the day had not been bad enough already, now he had lost communication with his deputies.

He looked up and jumped back as a car sped up to him, stopping just a few feet from him. Robert Hibbitts threw the door open and charged up to him.

"Sheriff! The school is on fire!"

"No, no, no....that was this morning. The alarms went off, but there was no fire."

"No! This time it IS on fire!"

"Did you call the Fire Department?"

"I tried but the phones are all out. I thought maybe you could radio them."

"Radio's out too. Let's go!"

They jumped into their vehicles and raced toward the Fire Department down the street. After a few seconds, Tim, Mr. Hibbitts and the firefighters all raced toward the school. A column of smoke rose from the cafeteria area as a group of onlookers gathered, all trying to use their phones but obviously failing. Several of them ran toward Tim's SUV.

"We were trying to call you. The phones aren't working!"

"Yes.... I know."

Flames shot out of the windows of the cafeteria. The firefighters broke down the doors and pulled their hoses in as fast as possible. A very thick smoke replaced the flames before long as Tim stood and watched with Mr. Hibbitts. He turned to the Principal and began to question him.

"Do you have any idea what started it?"

"No. We had just finished closing down the high school building for the early dismissal when we saw the smoke. Nobody was in there."

"Well, something started it. We'll have to check to see if it was arson."

They waited until the firefighters finished putting out the fire and came out to report to them. One of the firefighters, Kennith Perry, walked up to Tim and Robert.

"It started back in the kitchen area. I'm pretty sure it was arson because somebody had poured cooking grease onto a pile of boxes and apparently lit it up."

Tim scratched his head and stretched his neck to the side. "Who would do that?"

Kennith shrugged. "I'm pretty sure that will be up to your department to figure out."

"Great. Can we go in yet?"

"Yeah, but be careful. It's slick in there."

Tim and Robert picked their way to the back of the cafeteria and the kitchen area. Sure enough, a pile of burned cardboard sat in the middle of the floor, still smoking. Tim frowned and looked around.

"There's a hat over there. I wonder who that belongs to."

Robert picked it up and turned it over in his hands. I've seen this hat before, but I can't quite place the face that was under it. I'll ask the staff if they know."

Before Tim could comment, Oscar came running into the cafeteria yelling at Tim. "Tim! You've got to get over to Kinney...Now!"

"Why?"

"A damned fault line just opened up there!"

Tim frowned and rubbed his temples. He did not need to hear this right now.

"Oscar, I thought I just heard you say that a fault line just opened up in Kinney. Is that right?"

"Yes, Sir! Come on!"

Leaving Robert with the mystery of the hat, he ran out the door with Oscar and they hit the lights and sirens as they sped off to the Kinney subdivision.

Tim still could not wrap his head around it. "Was there an earthquake? I didn't feel one."

"Nope. It just opened up all by itself. A big old crack in the earth five feet wide and a couple of miles long. I was trying to call you but the radios aren't working."

"Yeah.... I know."

Once again, a large group of onlookers gathered at the beginning of the fault line, standing there entranced by the sight. Tim and Oscar got out of the SUV and walked toward them, sending the onlookers to a safer distance. He looked out at the group.

"Did anybody see this happen?"

Kat Merrill stepped forward. "Sheriff, I was the first one to find it. I was driving back home from the grocery store and had to stop because it went across the road. I didn't hear or see how or what happened."

"Anyone else?"

The bystanders all shook their heads. Tim rubbed his temples some more. His headache was getting worse.

"Oscar, get some police tape out here and let's get a couple of deputies out here to make sure nobody falls into that thing."

He turned and walked toward the vehicle. With all of this going on, he needed more coffee and his thermos was now empty. *And maybe I'll finally get something to eat. Burger Place time!*

THE HOLE IN THE SKY: PORTAL ONE

CHAPTER 18

Dana turned into the parking lot of the Burger Place and parked, sitting there for a moment with a blank stare as she absorbed the events of the day. She blinked her eyes and shook her head as she pulled the keys out of the ignition and stepped out of the car. Looking up, she noticed that the sky was darkening, even though she knew it was only late afternoon. She cast a glance toward the odd hole in the sky. Sure enough, bright beams of sunlight shone through the completely clear opening. She walked through the double glass doors and saw Debbie behind the counter with all her new injuries.

"Oh, my gosh! What happened to you?"

Debbie rubbed her arms and shuddered a bit. "I know you won't believe this, but all my cats attacked me when I went home. They've never acted like that before. And then they all ran away when I opened the door. They were acting strange this morning too. I don't know what got into them. But OUCH!"

Dana watched her intently as she told her what had happened. Somehow, it did not surprise her. Nothing could surprise her after today.

"They weren't rabid or something were they?"

"No, Ma'am. They all had their shots and they never go outside. But I have to admit, I thought about that too. They looked rabid. They weren't foaming at the mouth or anything, but the looks in their eyes were murderous. I was afraid they were trying to kill me."

"Well, be sure to put antibiotic ointment on those scratches so they don't get infected, especially with whatever it was that was wrong with them."

"Yes, Ma'am. I already did. I had a great science teacher who taught me that." She managed a faint smile. "What can I get for you?"

"Thanks, Debbie." Dana scanned the menu above. She was not particularly hungry, but she needed something. Something chocolate. Something dripping in chocolate.

"Hmm. How about a chocolate shake? No. Wait. A chocolate sundae with triple chocolate. Yes. That's what I need."

Debbie gave her a curious look. "Okay....Is everything alright with you, Mrs. Fleming?"

"Let's just say that I had an interesting day today, too. I just really need chocolate now."

Debbie gave her a knowing look and turned to prepare her order. Dana looked around the dining area. The glass panels that composed the outer walls of the Burger Place revealed that the sky was continuing to darken. She looked at her watch. *It's only four in the afternoon. There must be a storm coming.* Choosing a corner table, she sat down and waited for her sundae. She smiled as she watched Luke's old pickup turn into the parking lot. He entered the door, turned and waved to her and then continued to the counter to place his order. When he finished, he walked over to Dana's table.

"Mind if I sit here with you?"

Dana smiled. "No. Not at all. Have a seat."

He pointed to Debbie with his chin. "What happened to her?"

Debbie heard him. "My cats all attacked me this afternoon. They went crazy or something."

"Oh, man. I'm sorry to hear that. Make sure you put antibiotic ointment on those scratches."

"Yes, sir." She went back into the kitchen to start his order.

He turned back to Dana. "So, I hear that things at the school were a little wild again today."

Dana nodded. "You could say that. I'm over here because it drove me to my old nemesis...chocolate.

Luke laughed. "Yeah. They don't serve my nemesis here. So I guess I'll just have to have coffee with my hamburger."

Dana looked intently at him and did not say anything. Luke sat up straight in his chair in response. She decided that she had to share her terror with someone. And Luke seemed to understand the last time she had talked with him.

"What? What's that look for?"

"You know those coyotes you said you saw on your ranch? I think they came to my ranch too. Or maybe you put that in my head and I'm crazy enough to think I saw them."

"What do you mean? You saw them?"

Dana lowered her voice a bit. "Yeah. Both nights this weekend. And I think they were after my dogs. I had to bring them in. I saw the glowing eyes just beyond the fence."

Luke shook his head. "You're kidding, right? You saw 'em too?" He paused. "I don't want to know that."

"Why not?"

"Cuz that means they're real. As long as it's just me seeing 'em, I'm just crazy."

"If you're crazy because you saw them, then I'm crazy too. Well, that's what my daughter keeps telling me anyway. I believe 'certifiable' was her exact word."

Luke stared at Dana now. He did not want to know what she had just told him. And yet, he knew that the coyotes were real every time he saw the scratches on his truck.

Dana leaned in closer. "And that's not all. Something is in my house. Either that or I AM crazy. My keys keep moving and setting themselves up in the form of a tarantula. And something keeps unlocking my door every time I lock it. I don't mind saying that I'm scared."

They stared closely at each other for what seemed to be an eternity as they both realized that the terror they had been living through was real. Suddenly, headlights shone into the room through the glass walls.

THE HOLE IN THE SKY: PORTAL ONE

Luke turned his gaze away from Dana and glanced out the window. He cocked one eyebrow. "Looks like Tim needs something here, too."

Dana turned and watched as Tim's SUV came to a stop and he stepped out of it, looking rather haggard. "I'm pretty sure he's had a hell of a day today too. I saw him at the break of day handling that wreck. Did you see it?"

"Nope. I got there a little later. There was still shattered glass everywhere though. Terrible. Just terrible."

"And the gang fight earlier. I didn't know we had gangs. And then the school fire." She frowned. "What the hell is going on here?"

The bells on the door jingled as Tim entered the room. He waved at Luke and Dana and then stood at the counter waiting for Debbie. She came from the back and he frowned.

"What happened to you?"

Debbie sighed. "My cats. They attacked me. And no, I don't know why. And yes, I'm putting antibiotic ointment on the scratches."

He frowned again. "Okay. Sounds like you've had the same kind of day I've had."

"Yes, sir. I heard about your day. I'm amazed you are still standing. But, I always knew you were tough." She gave him a wink.

"Well, this 'tough' sheriff needs more coffee....a lot more coffee and a hamburger, because the fun just keeps happening. I just came from the fault line that opened up in Kinney."

Dana and Luke looked at him in surprise. Dana could not believe what she had just heard.

"Fault line? What fault line?"

"Yeah. I never knew there was a fault line there either. But today...there's a fault line. Don't ask me. Nobody felt an earthquake or anything. Though, it wouldn't surprise me if we had one of those today, too."

Dana knew that several of her students lived in Kinney. "Did anyone get hurt?"

"No. Not yet anyway. I left Shane and Kasey there to keep everybody out of it."

Before Tim could continue about the fault line, Ignacio drove up and parked. He struggled to get out of the truck and decided to leave his weapon there instead of having to fight with it with his broken arm. Dana, Luke and Tim all watched as he came through the door and waved at them before giving Debbie his order. Dana did not know that he had broken his arm.

"What happened to Ignacio's arm?"

Tim narrowed his eyes and lowered his voice. "He said he tripped over a trap and broke it. But, I still haven't figured out how that could happen."

Ignacio joined them at the table and Tim sat up and tried to act like he had not been talking about him.

"So, Ignacio, did you ever figure out what killed Billy's steer?"

Ignacio seemingly shuddered. "Uh.... no. I was thinking it was a mountain lion, but the tracks are all too small. I'm gonna have to put a camera out there at the kill."

Another set of headlights glared into the room as the Reverend Harris's SUV turned off the highway into the parking lot. His aide, Dan, left the vehicle running and stepped into the Burger Place. The group at the table watched as he nervously fumbled in his pockets for his wallet. Before he could even get his order made, a sudden squealing of tires in the parking lot drew their attention to the Reverend's SUV as it catapulted backwards at a high speed. The Reverend sat behind the wheel, glaring and smiling at them through the glass. He jerked the SUV around and peeled out of the parking lot, leaving Dan standing at the counter with his mouth open.

Tim jumped up. "What the hell is wrong with him?"

Dan turned and answered, "I... I wish I knew. But to be honest, I'm glad he's gone. He's been absolutely crazy today; even more crazy than before. I was worried that he was thinking about killing me."

Tim did not want to deal with it. "Then it's a good thing he's gone. He wouldn't dare try something with me sitting in here with you. Get your order and come have a seat."

Dan seated himself next to Dana and nervously looked around. "Well, I guess I should tell you what's been going on with him. The man is very sick."

He began to tell the group the whole story about the Reverend and his descent into insanity. Everyone listened attentively as he described the Reverend's nightly ritual of running all over the ranch barefooted and mostly naked.

"I've decided that he needs to be committed and I think he knows it. He's been glaring at me all day and I am serious when I say I think he wants to kill me. So, I may need your help soon, Sheriff."

Tim shook his head. "Sure. I can help you with that. But not today. All my deputies are very busy at the fault line and investigating the fire at the school. You might want to stay away from him until we can handle it."

Dan seemed relieved. "Yeah. I've decided not to go anywhere near him."

Debbie interrupted the conversation as she brought out the food and drinks for everyone. "Has anyone else noticed how dark it is out there? And it's only five. We must be about to have a storm."

Everyone looked out the glass windows and the conversation stopped as everyone ate their food and stared at the growing darkness.

Dana broke the silence. "Has anyone else noticed that there is no traffic on the highway?"

The group turned to look at the highway through the glass. The highway was always busy, so the absence of traffic made Tim frown. Had there been another wreck somewhere down the road that was blocking the traffic? Then, he realized that there would still be traffic coming from the other way.

Dana noticed something else. "And what's that orange glow to the west?"

They all got up and looked towards the west to see what Dana was talking about. The radiance did not emanate from the highway. Suddenly, Dana realized that it was coming from under that strange hole in the sky. *No. No. No. I am not going to do crazy now.*

A loud pop sounded and the lights went out. All the lights went out. Debbie ran from the kitchen and got as close to the group as possible. Tim instinctively put his hand on his gun, then realized what he was doing and let go of it.

Dana spoke out first. "It looks like they're out all over town. What could have done that?"

Tim tried to answer. "Maybe a transformer went out."

They stood there gazing out the window together as the orange glow reflected off of each of their faces. Suddenly, headlights appeared from the east. They all jerked their heads in that direction.

Dana made the observation. "That's the only car I've seen for at least an hour."

And it was not just any car. As the vehicle drew closer, they all saw that it was an SUV. The Reverend's SUV crept along the road at an agonizingly slow speed. As it approached the Burger Place, it did not turn into the parking lot, but continued along the highway slowly. Suddenly, the interior lights of the SUV turned on and everyone could make out the figure of the Reverend. Leaves and dirt covered his head and naked torso as he stared at the group and smiled.

Their mouths hung open as they watched him go by.

"Well, that wasn't creepy at all," Debbie uttered.

Tim decided that they all needed to calm down. "Let's just all have a seat and wait this out. All the radios and phones are dead. We might as well just stay here."

Debbie went to the kitchen to bring coffee. "It's cooler than normal, but it still has the caffeine."

They all sat down and tried not to panic. A dog wandered through the parking lot and up to the front door. It sat there and peered into the Burger Place, seemingly watching the group.

Dana thought it looked like it thought it belonged there. "Hey, Debbie. I think one of your 'babies' is here for his scraps."

"I don't feed any dogs."

"Well, this one sure looks like he thinks he's going to eat here."

As they sat there, another dog wandered up and joined the first one. They panted and wagged their tails at each other. Before too many minutes passed, another dog arrived and joined the other two.

Luke began to get nervous and he did not know why. His fidgeting caused Dana to look over at him.

"What's wrong, Luke?"

"I don't know. I don't like that the dogs are gathering here."

Another dog showed up and Luke could not stay seated. He got up and began to pace nervously in the dark room.

Tim finally asked him, "What's wrong, Luke?"

Luke hesitated. "Uh...nothin."

Dana knew why he was getting nervous. She was getting nervous, too. The dogs reminded her of all the stuff she had been going through at her house and she knew they reminded Luke of the coyotes.

Dana looked at Luke. "Just tell him. Tell him what happened out at your ranch! He needs to know."

Tim looked at Luke. "What do I need to know?"

Luke looked at Dana like she had slapped him. "No."

Dana stood up and grabbed his arm, stopping his pacing. "Come on, Luke, he'll believe you now. He's seen enough today that it'll make sense."

Luke looked at Dana and Dana nodded. "Go on. Tell him."

Luke took a deep breath and shrugged. "Okay. If you think I should."

He carefully explained each step of his discovery at his ranch and how he had barely gotten away with his life. The entire group listened intently. When he finished, the silence was intense as everyone continued to stare at him.

He turned to Dana. "See? They don't believe me."

Another dog joined the others.

Ignacio scooted his chair out. "As long as we are telling secrets, I have one too. I didn't fall over a trap and break my arm. I was attacked by a pack of huge bobcats."

He vividly described the bobcats and how the attack had happened as the others watched him carefully.

"There. Now you know. And to be honest, I'm scared to go back out there."

Another dog joined the pack outside. They danced around each other, jumping slightly up and down and yipping at each other in excitement.

"And those dogs out there are acting like a hunting pack. Just sayin'."

Dan shook his head. "I can't take any more of this. That's just ridiculous. All of it. If you don't mind, I'm going to my hotel room now."

He headed toward the door as all the others jumped up and started talking at once. Luke and Ignacio tried to stop him from going out the door, but he broke away from them, shaking his head as he opened the door. He took one step out the door.

The dogs leapt on him immediately, savagely growling and yipping and tearing his clothes and muscles. His piercing screams could barely be heard over the roar of the dogs growling. Tim reached for his gun and stepped to the door, shooting one of the dogs. The others stopped the attack momentarily, but then resumed it again even more ferociously. Tim shot several other dogs and the remaining dogs backed off for a moment. He grabbed Dan and pulled him back through the door. Another dog charged him and he shot it. He tried to shoot it again, but he was out of ammo. He quickly closed the door. The remaining dogs flung themselves onto the door, growling and scratching the glass hard. Luke stumbled backwards into the back wall, seemingly reliving his coyote encounter. Dana scrambled back there with him, pushing her body into his as close as possible and screaming loudly. Ignacio and Debbie stood there frozen with their eyes wide open. The sound of the dogs' teeth scraping on the glass and metal frames of the doors made them all shudder.

Dan moaned and Tim grabbed his belt to try to stop the bleeding. "Hey! I need another belt! He's bleeding to death!"

Luke snapped himself out of his panic attack and pulled his belt off to hand it to Tim. Tim worked feverishly to stop the bleeding.

Dana looked at Debbie, who was gagging from the smell of all the blood. "Get some clean towels! We need to put some pressure on those wounds."

Debbie ran to the kitchen and returned quickly with clean towels. More and more dogs joined the pack, surrounding the Burger Place and tearing at the building viciously. Tim and Luke worked on Dan trying to stop the bleeding, but before long, Dan stopped moaning and took his last breath lying in a pool of his own blood. Suddenly, a deafening silence surrounded them. They looked up. The dogs were gone.

Luke stared out the windows, shaking his head. "Just like the other night."

Dana stood up and grabbed his arm. "Come on, Luke. It's over."

"Is it? I'm not so sure. Yeah. It's over for Dan. But the rest of us.... well, that remains to be seen."

Tim laid some towels over Dan's bleeding face and pulled out his radio to try it once more. The static continued. He took his flashlight and aimed it outside the doors. Planters had been knocked over and the trashcan had fallen but everything else looked normal.

He turned to the group. "I think it's safe out there. It's like they just wanted Dan."

Dana shuddered. "He said the Reverend was trying to kill him. Looks like he succeeded."

Tim cautiously unlocked the doors and stepped outside. He swung the light from his flashlight all around and looked back at the others.

"Let's get out of here."

Dana looked up at Luke. "I don't want to go home alone. Will you come with me?"

Luke smiled. "Of course! I don't want to be alone either."

THE HOLE IN THE SKY: PORTAL ONE

CHAPTER 19

Luke practically had to fold in half to get into Dana's small car. She started it up and cautiously backed out of the parking place, glancing nervously around to make sure no dogs were in the area and clicking on the lights to see through the deepening darkness. As she pulled onto the highway, she looked over at Luke and smiled.

"I am so happy you're here with me. I'm frankly terrified. At least, if anything else happens, I'll know that I am not 'certifiable'."

Luke shifted in his seat. "Let's hope nothing else does happen."

"Agreed! The storm will pass and everything will go back to normal. Right?"

"Right."

As if on cue, the sound of what must have been all the dogs in town howling arose around them. They looked at each other. Within a few seconds, they reached the outer stretch of the road. Dana's eyes widened. There, on both sides of the road, the Watchers stood entranced as they gazed at the sky. When Dana followed their gaze, she realized that they were staring at the hole in the sky.

"Luke. Look at them! They've been acting so strange all day long. I actually heard them discussing something and using words that I know they don't know. They stayed in the school when everyone else left because of the fire drill. And now, look! What is wrong with those people?"

Luke shook his head. "That's not normal. What are they looking at?"

Dana shrugged. "I might as well tell you. It's weird, but you already know I'm weird. So...see that hole in the clouds?"

Luke looked up and frowned. "Yeah?"

"That thing is always there. It never moves. It's over a pasture on Dedra Boutwell's ranch. There's something very odd about that place and Dedra told me some fantastic things about it. And her daughters tried to have a party in the guesthouse there and something ran them out. I have to wonder if it has something to do with all this stuff that's happening."

"It appears to be in the area of the orange glow. But why is that family so entranced by it?"

"My question exactly."

Luke shook his head again. "I'm beginning to think we're starring in an episode of the Twilight Zone."

Dana nodded. "Yeah."

As they turned onto the road that Dana lived on, several coyotes could be heard howling loudly in every direction. Dana and Luke just turned and looked at each other. Dana took a deep breath.

"See why I didn't want to go home alone? I'm so glad you're here."

Luke took a deep breath and scanned the ranchland around him in the darkness. "Uhm. Yeah. Me too."

The sound of the caliche gravel under the tires of the car drove home the realization of the rural nature of Dana's house. They came around the curve of the driveway and Dana stopped for a moment. Darkness surrounded the house completely. She had not left any lights on in the house because she thought it would still be daylight when she got home.

She took a deep breath and continued up the drive towards the house. "Looks like I should've left some lights on. That's okay. I have a flashlight."

When they reached the house, she saw that Lola's car was there already. But why were all the lights out? "Hmm. Looks like Lola's car is here. She must have gotten a ride from someone and left her car here."

She collected the flashlight from the glove compartment and handed it to Luke. "Here. This will help."

The dogs started barking loudly and Dana tried to hush them. "It's okay... it's okay! It's just Luke. He's a nice person!"

Luke took Dana's arm and they walked together up the walk to the house. Dana fumbled with her keys and grabbed the door handle to unlock it. She tried to turn the lights on in the living room only to find that the electricity was out. They walked in and Dana reached back and locked the door.

"You saw me do that, right?"

"Right."

THE HOLE IN THE SKY: PORTAL ONE

Dana went to the stairs and called for Lola but got no reply.

"She must be out with her friends again. I wish I knew where she was. Especially today. No use trying to call her with all the cell phones out." She walked over to the kitchen. "I'm going to have some tea. You want some too?"

"That sounds good."

They walked into the kitchen and prepared the tea and went back out and sat down on the couch in the living room. Luke was looking around the room. Dana saw him and tugged on his shoulder.

"Do you want to see where I find the keys every day? I put them up on that counter over there, but I always find them right over there on the floor in front of the TV, standing on the tips of the keys like this." She folded her fingers into the tarantula formation. "And I've seen a black shadow figure over there."

The sound of footsteps on the stairs behind them made them jump and look quickly. Luke stood up getting ready to fight whatever was coming down the stairs. But they were surprised to see that it was Lola.

Dana frowned. "You were home? In the dark?"

Lola cocked her head at her mother. "I was taking a nap. What did you think I was, a ghost?" She shook her head at Luke. "See. My mom is crazy. She thinks we have ghosts and demons... oh, and coyotes with glowing eyes outside! Don't let her make you believe that stuff!" She took two more steps into the living room. "She is so crazy that she actually believes there is a God! Me? I'm sure she's having paranoid delusions."

Dana stepped towards her, frowning. "That's enough!" She turned to Luke. "Do you see what living with a teenager is like?" Luke stood there with his mouth open, not knowing what to say. "Luke, this is my daughter, Lola. Sometimes, she's much nicer than this."

Lola stomped her foot in anger and frowned. "I don't need this. I'll be upstairs in my room! Luke.... don't believe a word she says!" She stormed back up the stairs and they jumped at the sound of her bedroom door slamming.

Trying to be brave, Dana turned toward Luke and put her arms up in resignation. "I'm so sorry for that, Luke. We've been f....fighting...". The tears began to form in her eyes and, before she knew it, she was sobbing. She was so embarrassed and hurt again by the things her daughter said to her. Luke stepped forward and held her as she sobbed. He could not imagine having to live with someone like that. He felt so sorry for Dana and thought she really did not deserve such treatment. Everything he had seen in Dana so far had convinced him that she was a kind and intelligent woman.

He held her and began to stoke her soft hair. "It's okay. I don't believe her," he spoke into her ear softly. "You don't deserve that. You are a wonderful person."

She held tightly to him until the tears stopped flowing and then looked up at his kind face. "Thank you, Luke. That means so much to me." She pulled him down onto the couch and they sat very close to each other, looking intently at each other. She had not noticed how warm and inviting his dark eyes were until now. He still held her hand and she loved the feeling of it as it wrapped around her own hand. She had forgotten what it felt like to be held like that. And she had missed it.

Luke sat gazing into her tearful eyes. He felt the stirrings of feelings for her and that was a thing he thought he would never feel again. Could it be possible for him to have love again? The touch of her hand made him believe it could be, and it made him smile.

She sat up and looked carefully into his eyes. Maybe he would understand. "Am I such a horrible parent for believing in God?"

He smiled at her. "No. I think that makes you an incredible parent."

"Do you believe in God?"

He smiled again. "Yes. I think He's why I am still alive. I thought I was a goner when those coyotes attacked me. I'm sure He was responsible for them leaving me."

"I just have to wonder why we're going through all of this." Dana paused and then looked at Luke questioningly. "What about demons? Do you believe in demons? I mean, I think I've been seeing them. They look like dark shadows and they seem to be lurking everywhere."

"I did see something dark run behind a bush out at the ranch just before the attack. I thought my eyes were playing tricks on me. But, if you're seeing them too, that's probably what I saw." He paused. "And I think that, if there is a God, then all the stuff in the Bible is true and it talks about demons there. So, yeah...I believe in demons."

"What about angels? Have you ever seen an angel?"

"No. Can't say that I have. But I'm not sure what an angel would look like."

"I just think it's odd that we've seen the demons but not the angels. Why aren't they here protecting us?"

"I don't know. Maybe they are and we just can't see them."

"Well, I would like to see one. No. A bunch of them. Now. Then, I wouldn't be so scared."

"Until we do see one, we can help each other. Okay? I don't know about you, but I feel much better when I'm with you."

"Yeah. Me too. Your being here really helps. Thanks for coming out."

He gazed into her eyes and brushed her hair out of her face. She closed her eyes as he stroked his hand on her cheek. When she opened them again, she saw the gentlest look on his face. She reached up and touched his face. Then, she leaned forward and let her lips meet his. He responded by moving closer to her and wrapping his arms around her. The stress of the day left them both and they fell asleep holding each other close.

Lola crept out of her room and quietly closed the door behind her. She carefully avoided the parts of the stairs that squeaked when she stepped on them as she came down the stairs. All was quiet. She rounded the corner into the living room and saw her mother enveloped in Luke's arms. A quick look of disgust came over her face and she rolled her eyes. Tiptoeing down the hallway, she made it to the back door and slowly opened it to make her escape. She had to get away from that woman!

Closing the back door behind her, she looked out and quietly circled around the house to the driveway. She glanced behind her to make sure her mother had not awakened and noticed that she was gone. She had brought a flashlight, but did not really need it as the orange glow had intensified and she could see easily where she was stepping.

She quietly opened her car door and climbed in. Turning the keys in the ignition, she frowned. The car did not start. She tried it again with the same outcome. "Well, crap!"

She got out of the car and began to walk toward the highway. For the first time, she began to have a twinge of fear. She looked along both sides of the drive, instinctively fearing that she might actually see something. What if her mother was right about the coyotes with glowing eyes? *Pfff! What nonsense! Now she has me going crazy too!*

She stepped up her pace in anger at that thought, crunching the caliche under her shoes. As she approached the gate to the highway, a loud *snap* came from her right, just off the drive. She jerked her head in that direction to see what had made the sound and stopped walking. Staring into the darkness, she saw nothing. She took a deep breath and started walking again, scanning all around. A bush shook behind her and she wheeled around quickly. The bush moved as if something was behind it and she froze as she tried to catch a glimpse of what was causing it. Suddenly, a small, dark figure jumped slightly towards her. She screamed and then grabbed her mouth to silence herself. The armadillo looked as shocked to see her as she was to see him. She grabbed her chest and breathed hard, trying not to laugh at herself. *Ugh! Mother! See what you have done to me!*

She shook her head and headed forward in renewed anger. *I have GOT to get away from her!* Continuing to walk for a few more hundred feet, she heard a low growl emanate from the bushes along the side of the road just before her. After the last two panic attacks, she was determined not to react. "Yeah, yeah...whatever!" she said loudly, mainly to make herself feel better. But the growl only became louder and closer. She stopped and stared into the brush. The brush moved and twigs snapped. Her mouth fell open in true terror. The coyote stepped out from behind the brush, his eyes glowing and his fangs dripping. She began to hyperventilate as the beast stepped closer. She stopped breathing. Suddenly, the coyote turned his head towards something to the right and sat down.

Her eyes focused on whatever the coyote was looking at so intently, but saw nothing. Then, to her horror, she saw it. The darkness of the black shadow really stood out against the orange glow. She could see it plainly and make out its head and arms clearly. It stood glaring at her with red eyes. Again, she began to hyperventilate as it slowly moved towards her. It seemed to smile an evil smile. Several more coyotes began to surround her and she jerked her head in all directions, shaking violently as she looked at them.

The bushes rattled again to her left. She was sure that it had to be another coyote, but this time a man, or something like a man, stepped out from behind the brush. Leaves and twigs fell from his hair as he moved and what was left of his clothing barely clung to his bruised and scratched body. But that was not what terrified her the most. Crazed eyes squinted as he sneered at her. The shadows and the coyotes gathered around him and glared at her, snarling loudly.

Then, he spoke. "Ah yes...she will do quite nicely." And then she passed out.

In Dana's dream, she walked through her ranch in the dark towards the hole in the sky. As she reached the edge of the pasture, she looked up to examine the hole more closely. Inside the hole, glorious light shone brightly and yet did not hurt her eyes. She gazed at it and felt the warmth streaming from it. As she stood there, a stairway began to unfold toward the earth and the light from above spilled down on it. She spoke to herself in the dream. *Why, this is beautiful! Why would there be so much evil around here? Where is the evil coming from?* The ground around her began to tremble and turn orange in color. She turned as she heard the low rumble behind her and the ground began to shake violently.

A violent thrust pulled her out of her dream and she realized that everything around her was really shaking. Her quick glance around reminded her that she was in Luke's arms and she realized that he was still sleeping.

"Luke! Luke! Wake up! I think we're having an earthquake!"

Luke took a quick breath and opened his eyes, looking quickly around. "What the...."

"An earthquake! I think we're having an earthquake!"

Static filled the air and the smell of sulfur surrounded them. A sudden burst of lightening cracked just outside the window, sending Dana further into Luke's arms. She pulled back just enough to look into his eyes and see the terror there. The lights began to flicker and finally went out completely, leaving them in the darkness. Only it was not dark. The orange glow poured into the windows as the dogs began to howl. Coyotes nearby answered their howls. The screams of mountain lions and bobcats joined in harmony to them.

She broke loose of Luke's arms and ran quickly to the stairs. She had to get Lola and they had to get out of there. At the top of the stairs, she pushed Lola's door open. A sick feeling grew in her stomach. Lola was not there. "No!" She ran back down the stairs and looked all around. "Luke! She's gone! Where could she be?" Realizing that Lola was out there in the middle of the earthquakes and lightening, she screamed, "No, no, no!" She raced over to the windows and looked out. Lola's car was still there. "There is her car! How did she go anywhere?"

Luke grabbed her. "Calm down. We'll find her. Get your keys. She can't be far."

Dana reached for the keys and realized that they were not on the counter where she had left them. She quickly turned towards the TV and pointed her finger. "See, Luke? Just like I said." The keys lay on the floor by the TV in the tarantula formation. She scooped them up and ran to the door. It was unlocked. "It's unlocked! And you saw me lock it!"

"Maybe Lola unlocked it."

"We would have heard it. It makes a lot of noise when you unlock it. I'm pretty sure she went out the back door so we would not wake up. Come on! Let's go!"

As they ran out the door, Dana realized that Sam and Buddy were nowhere to be found. She could not worry about that now. They climbed into her car. She put the key into the ignition and turned it, but nothing happened. "Oh, great! Let's try Lola's car." She tried Lola's car, but it would not start either.

Luke looked at her. "We'll just have to walk. Lola's walking too so maybe we can catch up to her if we hurry." He looked up. "Oh, wow.... look at that!"

Dana followed Luke's gaze. A red hue had replaced the orange glow from before and a mist had begun to form just under the hole in the sky. Looking down the caliche road, she realized that it would take far too long to catch up with Lola if they walked the drive and then turned onto the highway. They would have to cut across the ranch.

"We have to go this way. We'll find her faster."

She grabbed Luke's hand and pulled him along onto a path into the pasture. Instinctively, she knew that Lola would be at the pasture under the hole in the sky. They had to hurry. The thorns on the cacti and catclaw brushes ripped at her pants leg and penetrated a few times through the clothing, tearing at her skin. But she did not slow down. They pushed through the brush until they came to a fence. Luke held the wire down for Dana to step over and followed easily with his long legs.

Just as they approached the road, they stopped short. Looming in front of them were two black shadows, glowering at them with their red eyes. Dana moved closer to Luke's side and grabbed his waist.

"Oh, God! What do we do?"

Luke held her tight. "I don't know. Pray?"

She looked up at him. She had not thought of that. But she realized that praying was their only option. She could not get through the demons to get to Lola and God was her only way. "Yes. Let's pray. Now."

"I don't know what to say."

All of the terrors Dana had lived through began to play through her head. It had all come to this. Nothing she could do could save her daughter. Maybe she had to go through it all just to realize that God was her only salvation. "Luke," she said softly. "We are powerless. Do you feel it?"

Luke squeezed tighter. His voice faltered a bit as he answered, "You're right. We're done unless we get some help."

Dana looked up into the orange sky and began to sob. "Oh my God...please help us now. Forgive me for not trusting you with everything. Forgive me for blaming you. Forgive me for hating Lola. Forgive me for everything." She wept loudly and her chest began to heave in heavy sobs as she knelt down on one knee. "Oh my God...save us now. Save Lola now. Help us find her. And protect her with your angels." Her voice broke. "Please." She bowed her head down and lay in a crumpled heap, sobbing uncontrollably.

Luke's eyes began to fill with tears at the sight of Dana so broken. "Lord. Forgive me for everything and for not coming to you sooner. Please help us now. You are our only hope." He kneeled down and put his arms over Dana, now sobbing along with her.

The air around them began to hum with a sound similar to electricity. They stopped crying and Luke held Dana tighter, thinking that the demons were upon them. Luke looked up. He tugged on Dana's shoulder.

"Look!"

Dana looked up and her mouth fell open. She fell back into a sitting position and watched in shock as the orbs began to circle around them. Hues of blue, red and purple along with pink seemingly washed over the orbs in flowing waves of shimmering spray. The edges glowed and streamed like waves on the ocean. The orbs floated gracefully above them and soared and dipped in beautiful harmony. Dana jumped back.

"Watch out!" She was sure that these orbs had to be the very same orbs that had attacked the girls at the party. She held her breath as she waited for them to attack. But something about them calmed her as she watched them. How could something so beautiful be so evil? The orbs began to move toward the demons and the demons backed up. The orbs closed in on the demons and the demons turned and fled. Dana and Luke sat there in amazement at the sight. As soon as the demons left, the orbs shot up into the night toward the hole in the sky.

"Did you see that?" Dana squealed. "They ran off the demons!"

"Yeah. They did!"

Dana stared off into the direction that the orbs had gone. "Those had to be the Marfa lights that Dedra said were in her pasture. I mean, they look exactly like what she described."

"Marfa lights? Here?"

"Yeah. Dedra said they have lights just like the Marfa lights in the pasture under the hole in the sky. They came over here and they scared off the demons. It makes no sense though. The orbs attacked a group of my students in Dedra's guesthouse when they were having a party. I thought they were evil, but maybe not."

Luke rubbed his chin and shook his head. "Anything that can run off demons is not evil. There must have been some other reason they came into the house. I don't know about you, but I'm pretty sure they were on our side."

"You're right. I'm glad they showed up when they did." She paused. "Maybe God sent them."

"I've never heard of such things though. I'm tellin you we're in some kind of Twilight Zone episode. But, we have to keep going. Maybe God will help us find Lola."

They moved even faster now, renewed with hope. A slight brushing feeling slipped across Dana's foot and she looked down to see what it was, but it was too quick and it was gone.

"Did you see what that was?"

"No. What happened?"

"Something just ran over my foot."

"Maybe it was a bug."

"It was too big to be a bug."

Dana began to keep an eye on her feet as she walked. She felt the sensation again but this time she saw what had crossed over her foot. "Aaaaah! A snake! A snake slithered across my foot!"

Luke quickly looked down and realized that he had a snake going across his boot too. "What the...!" He started hopping around with Dana as several other snakes brushed past them. Then, he stopped and stood still. "They don't even care if we're here. They're all going somewhere in a hurry."

Dana shuddered. "Yes.... toward the hole in the sky."

They relaxed a bit and gingerly walked among the racing snakes, holding on to each other for balance on the moving ground. The ground was moving because of the snakes and because of constant tremors. Lightening pierced the red color of the night.

Luke shook his head. "What in tarnation has gotten into them? I've never seen such in all my years at the ranch."

Dana pointed to the hole in the sky. "It's that! That's what's causing everything. We have to get there. I feel like Lola is there."

"Yeah. Let's go."

They moved carefully through the brush, keeping their eyes open for any more demons. Dana kept glancing down at her feet nervously now with every sensation. The number of snakes passing them decreased a bit but then she noticed something else moving in the direction of the hole in the sky. She squinted to make sure she was not seeing things. She began to jump around again.

"Luke! Scorpions! Thousands of them!"

Luke jerked his head down to confirm the reason for her panic. He took a deep breath and held it. Sure enough, a stream of scorpions raced past them in the same direction as the snakes. "Oh, man! It's like every creepy thing out here is doing their damnedest to get over there!" He watched them for a few seconds. "But I don't think they're interested in us. Just keep going...try to ignore them."

Dana shuddered. She hated scorpions. And the crunching beneath her feet reminded her with every step that scorpions surrounded her. "Ugh!" But the thought of Lola being out there somewhere in all of this by herself drove her on despite the inward revulsion she felt.

A low growl caused her to gasp. She tugged hard on Luke's arm. "Did you hear that?"

"Yeah. I did."

They crept forward, searching all around for the source of the sound. They did not have to search for long. Standing immediately in front of them were two huge coyotes with their heads lowered and their glowing eyes locked on Dana and Luke as they intensified their menacing growls. Luke nearly choked and stepped falteringly backwards at the sight. Dana grabbed his arm. She knew that his fear of these creatures could cripple him and she needed him to be strong now.

"Luke.... they aren't any worse than the demons. Let's ask God to deal with them."

Luke kept his eyes squarely on the intimidating sight before him. "O...Okay."

Dana began to pray. "My Father. You saved us before. Please save us now. You are our only hope."

"A... amen."

The coyotes stepped closer to them. Luke felt his knees begin to buckle slightly, but Dana's grip on his arm braced him and he managed to keep standing. "So... where is the rescue?"

Dana began to cry. "I don't know." A sudden realization came over her. God apparently wanted them to be safe or He would not have run off the demons. Somehow, she knew He would not abandon them now. She stood up straight and faced the coyotes. She took a step towards them. They snarled and bared their huge canines, licking and snapping at her. Luke reached towards her in panic.

"Dana! What are you doing? Get back!"

She took another step towards them and the growling intensified. She narrowed her eyes as she spoke to them. "You must leave!" she shouted loudly at them. "God is my defender and He will not let you hurt us."

The coyotes began to blink as she spoke these words and it gave her courage. "Get out of our way or we will call on God and he will send the orbs to attack you!" Just as she had spoken these words, they felt the electric static sensation they had felt before and looked up. Three orbs floated above them. The coyotes snapped their jaws at the orbs but the orbs began to move towards them. Finally, the coyotes turned and fled in the direction of the hole in the sky. Dana exhaled and Luke turned towards her in relief. Dana looked deep into his eyes.

"See? He's helping us. He sent the orbs! He wants us to save Lola."

"Are you crazy? Don't ever do that again!"

"I don't know how but I knew it would be alright." She rubbed her temples. "Maybe that is what they call faith."

"Or stupidity! You could have been killed. They're vicious killers."

"Apparently, they are not as ferocious as God."

Luke shook his head. She was right. She reached for his arm and pulled him forward.

"Let's go."

They held onto each other as they trudged towards the red light. Crossing the highway, Luke once again lowered the fence for Dana and they scrambled up a slight hill. They stepped out of the brush. And fell onto their stomachs.

The sight before them caused their mouths to fall open. A ridge rose up out of the pasture and small streams of lava poured down around it in several places. A slight knoll stood between them and the ridge and Dana and Luke could see people lying on their stomachs like they were. Dana strained to recognize who it might be.

She had to shout because a roaring sound emanated from the ridge. "Who is that, Luke? Can you make it out?" Her breath became mist with each syllable.

Luke struggled to recognize who was there because of the intense red light in front of them. He thought he could pick out Tim's hat. "I think I see Tim, or at least his hat. That could be Oscar beside him. Let's move closer."

They stood up and bent over as they ran up the knoll. Approaching it, they could plainly make out Tim and Oscar. On all sides of them, others lay peeking over the knoll. Ignacio leaned on his good arm and Dana's students, April, Heather and Savannah lay next to him. Dana and Luke scooted up behind Tim and Luke tapped him on the shoulder. Tim jumped and grabbed his gun, pointing it at them. Then, he exhaled and put it down.

"Oh, my God! Don't do that!"

Luke shrugged. "Sorry. What's going on? What in the hell is that?"

Dana and Luke tried to take it all in as they lay down along side of Tim and the others. From their position on the knoll, they could see clearly what was happening under the hole in the sky. Mutated coyotes ringed the entire edge of the ridge. They howled loudly over and over. Mutated bobcats punctuated the cacophony with screams as they stood along with the coyotes. The ridge appeared to be moving as the snakes slithered en masse along it under the feet of the coyotes and bobcats along with the hordes of scorpions and other insects. Other snakes stood straight on their tails, as if at attention, between the coyotes. Beneath them, inside the ridge, the red lava boiled, sending puffs of red mist up toward the hole. Some of the puffs of mist formed into giant claws as they stretched upwards. Apparently, all of the dogs and cats from the city had made it to the volcano as they made up the lowest layer below the coyotes. Silhouettes of thousands of vultures punctuated the limbs of the trees all around the area.

Tim shook his head. "I don't know. Haven't been able to get a hold of anybody. All the phones and radios are useless. I don't know if this is only happening here or if it's everywhere. As far as I know, this could be the end of the world." He turned back to observe the ridge again.

Luke gave Dana a nervous glance. Dana put her hand on his face and then turned back to the ridge. A clap of thunder sounded and she shrieked and then held her hand to her mouth. Luke followed her gaze. Just under the ridge, a group of coyotes stepped from the other side of the ridge, followed by several demons and the Watchers....escorting Lola's limp body. Her still form seemingly floated above the ground behind the coyote and demon escort. Behind her appeared the naked figure of the Reverend. His hysterical smile could be seen clearly even at that distance. The entourage began to turn up towards the edge of the ridge as lightening danced around them.

Dana grabbed Luke in a panic. "He has her! Do something!"

Luke elbowed Tim. "That's Lola, Dana's daughter. We have to save her."

Tim looked at him. "Got any ideas?"

Dana scrambled over Luke and got into Tim's face. "You have to do something! It looks like he's planning to throw her in the volcano!"

Tim frowned. "We sent Shane over there a little while ago. That's his body.... see it? I don't know what to do."

Dana realized that, once again, it looked like there was no hope. She paused. Then, she remembered how she and Luke had been saved. She looked into Tim's eyes. "We can pray... all of us together!"

Tim eyed her for a second and then nodded. He motioned to the others and they all held hands. Then, he motioned to Dana.

Dana knew that all of her life had led to this moment. The prayer she must offer now would be the only hope for Lola. She began to sob and shake. "My Father...please hear my plea. You alone are able to save Lola from them. Please...please... I beg you, Father!" The others all nodded and said, "Amen."

She quickly glanced back at the volcano and saw that the Reverend stood perched at the edge of it, holding a knife in his hand as he raised it up. Dana could not believe what she was seeing. It was as if he was sacrificing Lola to the volcano. "Please, God, Please!"

A white mist began to flow from the hole in the sky, downward toward the evil horde below. Suddenly, thousands of orbs poured from the hole. The first orbs zoomed toward the Reverend, engulfing him in a brightly-colored casing. Dana could not see through them to know what was happening. She stood up in the hopes of seeing better but it did not help. A loud scream pierced through the noise, followed by a splash and a sudden burst of steam as something fell into the lava below.

Dana fell to her knees. "Please, God, Please!"

Suddenly, Lola's body rolled down the edge of the volcano toward Dana and the others. It came to a stop and landed in a heap. Dana began to sob. "No. No. No." But, the heap jumped up and began to run toward them. Lola ran for her life away from the creatures of evil behind her. Several orbs followed behind her, in escort, as she scrambled up the little knoll, screaming. April ran toward her and took her arm to pull her up. Dana grabbed her, sobbing uncontrollably now, and held her shaking body.

"I've got you. I've got you. It's okay. I've got you."

Lola held tightly to her mother as Luke, Tim and the girls crowded around them. "I'm so sorry, Mom...you were right." She leaned back and looked at her mother through the tears. "I should have listened to you! You're not crazy." She grabbed Dana and held her tightly. "I love you, Mom."

Dana brushed the hair out of her face. "It was God who saved you, not me. I just prayed and He did it."

Lola looked up at the orbs. "Mom, I think those are angels. God sent his angels to save me...Thank you, God!" She wept loudly as she held her mother tight.

"I think you're right. They are angels."

They turned to look back at the volcano. More and more orbs flew through the hole and encircled it as the creatures looked up in panic. The sound of wings could be heard now and it grew more intense as the number of orbs increased exponentially. The screeching of the demons along with the howling and screams of the animals built to a crescendo as a thick white mist flowed heavily from the hole. The mist formed into a hand and grabbed the entire edge of the volcano. It squeezed hard and a loud hissing sound escaped as steam rose up and lava flowed through the fingers of the hand. Then, the hand formed into a fist and pushed the volcano down. Lava ran everywhere as did the animals around the volcano. The Watchers turned away from the volcano and stumbled down the edge of it, rubbing their eyes in confusion. Just as Dana and Luke were thinking they should leave, a very cold wind began to blow from the hole and the lava instantly hardened with a deafening cracking sound. The red mist transformed into blue swirls under the hole. The orbs began to ascend through it and, as the last one passed the entrance, the hole in the sky closed.

Silence engulfed the group.

They stood in amazement at what they had just witnessed. Nobody said a word. Suddenly, a loud crackle broke the silence as Tim's radio came to life. He looked down at it in confusion and then pushed the button to talk.

"Say again? Do you read?"

"Ten-four. What is your status?"

Dana and Luke embraced and kissed for several seconds as Lola watched uneasily. She put her hands on her hips.

"Mom! Really?"

Dana pulled one arm away from Luke and extended it to Lola. Lola ran to join them and they held each other as they cried happy tears. They suddenly heard barking and turned to see Buddy and Sam racing to join them in the glad reunion.

The sun rose slowly from the East as Tim and Oscar led a group of scientists from San Antonio to the location of the last night's events. Tim sighed and rubbed his weary eyes. He knew nobody would believe what they had witnessed. But, the authorities had been notified by someone at the nearby Air Base that seismic activity had occurred in the location. Tim gave Oscar a look and Oscar shook his head. Should they try to tell them what had happened? They reached the site on the Boutwell Ranch. Tim had hoped that the morning sun would reveal more evidence than they had been able to find in the dark. But the serene appearance of the scene belied the events from the night before. All of the bodies of the killed animals and even Shane's body had been swallowed up in the volcano.

Dr. Samantha Vargas, Chief Researcher for Upton Geological Services, stopped as she noticed the cooled lava bed. She looked over to her assistants, Dr. Joseph Haynes and Dr. Mark Walsh. "That is obviously cooled lava. But I sincerely doubt that it was liquid last night. It takes much longer to cool into this state."

Tim shuffled his boot and looked up into the sky, trying not to say what he wanted to say. Oscar just turned away.

Dr. Vargas knelt down and felt of the rock. "It does show some powerful cracking. Like it cooled very quickly." She looked up at Tim. "Like a warm glass shattering under a stream of cold water."

Tim nodded knowingly and smiled. "Do you think it is related to the fault I just showed you at Kinney?"

"Could be. But something obviously happened here. The last time I saw anything thing like this was in Hawaii. But you don't have any active volcanoes in this area so it makes no sense."

Tim and Oscar looked at each other in confirmation of their pledge to each other not to tell anyone what they had seen. Then, they each planted a pleasant smile on their faces as the scientists went about their work debunking that anything major had occurred there. *No. No. No...Not crazy...*

Susan closed her eyes and listened to the soothing sound of the waves lapping up on the shore next to her small home on the coast of Washington State. Breathing in the salty air, she relaxed and then opened her eyes. A small frown formed on her brow. She spoke into the wind. "Well...that's been here for the last few evenings. I wonder what it is." She cocked her head as she tried to inspect the odd formation in the clouds. "I never noticed that before this week. Hmm. So that little place over the ocean wants to be clear when it's cloudy everywhere else."

If you enjoyed reading this book, please consider leaving a good review on Amazon.com and sharing your enthusiasm on your social media sites. Also check out........

Weapon of Jihad

https://www.amazon.com/Weapon-Jihad-revised-political-biowarfar/dp/0983668007/ref=sr_1_1?ie=UTF8&qid=1491596928&sr=8-1&keywords=weapon+of+jihad

Growing Up Weird: Confessions of a Closet Medium

https://www.amazon.com/Growing-Up-Weird-Confessions-Closet/dp/0983668015/ref=sr_1_1?ie=UTF8&qid=1491597077&sr=8-1&keywords=growing+up+weird

Thank you!